THE OATH

Susan S. Maire

August 21th, 1066
Ghent, Flanders

I sat at the back of the courtroom watching as the final act of William and Harold's battle regarding the sovereignty of England began.

Whump! Whump! Whump! The contact resonated within the stately chambers, the court bailiff striking the floor with his staff after the final blow crying the traditional invocation, "Oyez, Oyez, Oyez. All persons having business before the Honorable, the Justices of the Court of Justice of the Association of International Communities are admonished to draw near and give their attention, for the Court is now sitting. God save the Association of International Communities and this Honorable Court."

The twelve judges solemnly filed into the cathedral-like courtroom. Habited in their black robes and white lace jabots, they created an aura of stateliness and morality as they took their places at the long, high bench crowned by the stained glass windows. Chief Justice Di Vinci—appointed by Domenico Contarini, Doge of Venice—gave permission for all to sit, and began the ritual of introducing each of the justices. Each justice had been appointed by the king or similar leader of the counties or territories from which they came. Each was a leading jurist of that member state of the AIC.

Chief Justice Di Vinci administered to them the oath to judge fairly in the matter now before them, of William, Duke of Normandy versus Harold II, King of England.

While the judges were being introduced, I watched my uncle, the defendant King Harold II, sitting anxiously at Defendant's table with his brother Leofwine as his counsel. I knew how hard he was trying to convey the same aura of stateliness and justice as this magnificent hall exhibited, although I was well aware that he was far from feeling either. So much was at stake here, the very future of England.

While the opening protocols droned on, I couldn't help but recall the events leading up to this trial, which had been set in motion long before that January night eight months ago when King Edward died and my uncle became Harold II, King of England.

I was only a child when the Archbishop of Canterbury—Robert of Jumièges, more politician than prelate—spirited my uncle Wulfnoth, King Harold's youngest brother and me to Duke William's court. I learned later that it had been the Archbishop who orchestrated the earlier actions of King Edward, forcing the Godwine family into a position opposing the king which resulted in their exile. Robert of Jumièges had also persuaded the King to send Queen Edith to a nunnery. His aim was to have King Edward divorce her, get Edward married to a Norman or at least someone Robert could control and get an heir who would not be a Godwine. The Archbishop wanted no more Godwines in positions of power that could challenge his influence upon the King.

Wily as the Archbishop was, he had not been prepared for the outcry by the English at the appointment of a Norman as Archbishop of Canterbury. When my grandfather and uncles re-entered England in force the following year, they were widely supported. King Edward admitted defeat and restored all their lands. The Witan outlawed Archbishop Robert, and he and many other Normans fled to Normandy. Unfortunately for me and Wulfnoth, when he fled, he abducted us and took us with him. At six years old, I didn't have any say in the matter, and Wulfnoth, even though older, had no opportunity to resist our sudden abduction either.

Uncle Harold's decision to seek Wulfnoth and my release wasn't wrong in itself, just the way it turned out, except for me, I got to return to England. It was as if the gods were lounging around one day bored, with nothing to do and one of them said, "I know. let's go play with mortals!"

And another said, "Okay but which ones?"

"Close your eyes, turn around three times and point and those will be the ones we play with," came the reply.

So the god closed his eyes, turned three times and pointed to the English Channel.

"Oh, that's no fun" said a god, "that's just water."

"But it's a nice day there, some boats with mortals are sure to be on the water," joined in another.

"How about we send a swift summer squall along the coast of northern France and see what happens?"

Which they proceeded to do. And Uncle Harold, who was one of those hapless mortals, instead of a pleasant sail to Flanders and visit with Count Baldwin to seek his help in approaching Duke William, Harold ended up shipwrecked on the coast of Ponthieu, France. Guy, Count of Ponthieu, quickly took Harold and his men into custody to hold for ransom.

In the usual course of events, the Godwines would have been apprised of the ransom demand, paid it and Harold and his men would have gone home. But the gods weren't finished with their game of mortals, so they introduced another quirk of fate to the game: they made sure William Duke of Normandy heard of Harold's capture.

William, urged by the gods, immediately rode to Ponthieu and demanded that his vassal Count Guy, turn Harold and his men over to him. Earl Harold and his men became the unwilling *guests* of Duke William until such time as William decided to allow them to return to England, and provided the means to do so. And I met my uncle again for the first time in twelve years!

I was there when my uncle's naiveté led him to be maneuvered into taking an Oath of fealty to William. That oath could well be the critical issue that would tumble his reign and give William the throne of England! Now that was a thought enough to have even my stomach in a turmoil. Twelve years as William's *guest* had taught me well that I didn't want to be anywhere near William ever again.

I now knew my uncle well since I had been living in his household since my return from Normandy. I knew that while sitting at that table with such apparent calm, his thoughts were racing in circles questioning over and over, could such a reasonable endeavor -to seek the release of a brother and nephew from their enforced stay in Normandy as hostages for the good behavior of a man now dead, possibly have resulted in this moral and political fiasco?

Across the aisle at Plaintiff's table William, Duke of Normandy—also known as William the Bastard—sat with his counsel, Richard Vos: Vicomte de Conches en Ouches.

After fourteen years as his hostage, I was very familiar with William the Bastard of Normandy. It had been two years since I had been released from his custody. My uncle Wulfnoth, Harold's youngest brother, had not been so lucky. He was still retained as William's *guest*. Duke William certainly looked confident, but then he was arrogant enough to believe that whatever he wanted, would come to pass. And he had decided he wanted England. Never mind that England didn't want him or any other Norman foreigner as its king!

Now, here we all were, before this international court, William seeking a decision that he, not Harold, should be the King of England. What if this Court were to believe William's tale of half-truths, innuendos, and outright lies? He could be so convincing! It just might happen!

January 3d, 1066
London, England

Recalling the fateful events of the past ten days, I couldn't help but notice the difference between Christmas at King Edward's court this year from that of last year. A year ago had been my first Christmas home in twelve years. It was a bright, sunny and definitely merry holiday season. As usual many of the powerful people of the kingdom had come to London to enjoy the holidays with the King's court. There had been hunting, feasting and in general, merrymaking. It was also the occasion for the meeting of the Witenagemot, the council of the King's advisors.

One year later, in the gray mist of a January day, the damp chill seeking the marrow of our bones, I watched Uncle Harold Godwineson's long stride crunch against the gravel of the garden's meandering path. He and his brother Leofwine were taking a respite from the tensions of the vigil at King Edward's bedside, escaping the cloying, claustrophobic atmosphere of the King's chamber, the smells of illness and impending death. And the whispered scheming and positioning of powerful men in the event of the King's death, which was likely.

As usual, Harold was elegantly and fashionably dressed. But even his stylish cloak trimmed with fur didn't seem to keep out the cold thoughts squirreling around in his head. His mind in a turmoil, he paced the garden's paths, Leofwine hurrying to keep up, with him and me following in attendance should he want anything.

"Edward has had relapses similar to this before, Leofwine, but it seems unlikely he will survive this one. If he doesn't, what will happen to England? Edward has no children. Everyone acknowledges Edgar the Aetheling's status as Atheling to claim the throne, even though technically he isn't an Aetheling, *one worthy to be king* since his father wasn't a king. But I suppose Edward's decision that he be considered an Aetheling amounts to his adoption, so I guess that makes it alright. Clearly he is of the royal Saxon house of Edmund Ironsides. But he is only twelve years old, with no training, and he barely speaks English or French. How can England survive a child king?

As he wearily sat on one of the benches provided along the paths, he continued, "If the Atheling takes the throne, there will have to be a regent. We both know that our sister Edith, as Queen, would insist on being the only regent. I wouldn't agree to that and I don't think the Witen would either. But they might allow a co-regency, if the other regent were me. Edith still has not forgiven me for agreeing with Northumbria that our brother Tostig be removed as its earl. She would be difficult to work with as a co-regent, but with the support of the Witen, it could be done. I would be mainly concerned that she would try to have Tostig forgiven and recalled, to have him as an ally if not as co-regent. If he returns triumphant from exile, could England survive his influence on Edith? He may be our brother but he is a hot-headed, spoiled brat that always blames someone else for the problems he creates."

Leofwtne had no answers to any of these questions but he knew Harold wasn't truly looking to him for answers, only to be able to vent his concerns to someone he trusted.

"What will happen when King Harald Hardrada of Norway tries to reclaim England from when Canute was its king?" Harold queried. "He appears to be getting ready to include England as part of his Scandinavian empire. Particularly if we have an inexperienced minor for a King.

"A Witenagemot is present right now for the Christmas festivities and the consecration of Westminster Abbey. It is especially important these leading earls and prelates of the country are all here now, since it is unlikely Edward will survive this relapse. The Witan members are urging me to accept the crown when Edward dies. They are well aware that as Earl of Wessex, I have been *sub-regulus*, the power behind Edward during these past several years of his reign. As Edward has retreated more and more into a pious, monastic lifestyle, and bouts of illness, the reins of government have had to be held by me."

"I know, and I firmly agree with the other earls," Leofwine replied. "Those who are aware of Duke William of Normandy's claim to the throne are adamant that a Norman could never be their king. The memories of the favoritisms Edward has given to his Norman friends and the havoc it caused is still fresh in their minds. None of the prelates and earls with whom I have spoken, will have any part of a bastard Norman Duke as king."

Harold's thoughts about the succession bounced back and forth like drops of oil on a hot skillet. He wasn't of a royal line except distantly by marriage. But neither was he a bastard. Of course, many of the English were of Scandinavian bloodlines, still, did anyone want England to become a vassal province of Harald Hardrada's Norway? Not many.

Who was left who could deal with the threat his brother Tosig presented? The only one who could have was their father, Godwine, and he was dead. Tostig had no compunctions about starting a civil war to gain what he wanted namely—

Northumbria—under his control. Or even better, in the case of a regency, as co-regent with Dowager Queen Edith.

Among all these other worries, what really concerned him was the Oath of fealty he had given William. No one had actually heard the words William had said, or that Harold said, except William's court had seen Harold stand bare-headed before William, with his hands on the altar and Holy relics, and take some kind of oath. However, he knew what he had sworn. He knew he had sworn an oath of fealty, a pledge of allegiance to William. But had he any choice? Nephew Harkon and his own youngest brother Wulfnoth were William's prisoners! There was no means of returning to England unless William allowed it and provided transportation for him and his men. Was there any way to keep his oath to God and still protect England? Surely God couldn't be asking him to desert England when it needed him the most?

Although his thoughts circled round and around, his sense of duty and honor were slowly but surely spiraling his deliberations to a conclusion that he had no choice. Beset as the country was from all sides, there was no one else who had the power, the knowledge, and experience; no one else to lead England at this time with any hope of its survival as a nation.

"I don't seem to have much choice do I, Leofwine? If I accept the Witan's urgings, we need to be certain that the earls of Northumbria and Mercia concur in the decision. England must be united if it is going to survive these challenging times. Neither Earl is inclined to view with favor any member of the Godwine family, especially if it means a further increase in power."

"Well," said Leofwine, "think about this. You know that as king, you will have to have a wife/queen bound to you by a Christian church ceremony. I know how you feel about Edith, but a hand-fast marriage won't be acceptable for a king. Isn't

Mocar's sister, Ealdgyth, now a widow? Close family ties make for good alliances."

Accepting that Leofwine's proposal made great sense, and was certainly worth considering, Harold and Leofwine returned to Harold's chambers to set about putting his recommendation into effect. Harold sent me to find messengers to locate Earl Mocar and Edwin to ask that they join him in his chambers and see that servants brought food and drink for the meeting.

As these preparations were made ready, Harold wondered whether the earls would even consider this proposed alliance. As he knew, neither was a fan of the Godwine family. Morcar, now Earl of Northumbria, had led the revolt against Tosig Godwineson. Edwin, his brother and Earl of Mercia, had supported him. However, the assent of the earls of the North had to be secured before talking further with the other earls and prelates of the Kingdom.

When they arrived shortly thereafter, Harold wasted little time in pleasantries. "Mocar, Edwin, I'm sure you are aware of the urgings of the other earls and prelates for me to accept the crown upon Edward's death. I don't believe anyone thinks that in these troubled times, we can survive with a child king. Having been the sub-king for the past several years, I am considering their urgings. If I accept, will you oppose it?"

"I will if it means I have to surrender Northumbria to another as Earl," Mocar challenged.

Edwin chimed in, "The North has managed to rule itself for generations without interference from the South. We would keep it that way."

"England must stand united in these times. The country cannot afford to give in to disputes that would have us arguing among ourselves, to be picked off separately by our enemies," Harold replied.

Rising from his seat and offering each man a goblet, Harold continued, "As you know Mocar, I supported you to Edward against my own brother. I urged and recommended to Edward that it would be in the best interests of the North and England if you both remained earls in the North. With you each as earl, it would ensure that the traditional customs and practices of the North would remain in place and restore peace to the North. I have not changed my mind about this. I also ask that you also consider the advantages of even closer ties with the House of Godwine. If I become King, I will need a church-wed wife. Your widowed sister, Ealdgyth, now lives with you, doesn't she? She would be a very suitable consort."

The negotiations between the earls continued for several hours, ending in agreement that the northern earls would support Harold as King Edward's successor and Ealdgyth would become Harold's wife and queen.

After the meeting, Leofwine and Harold discussed what had been accomplished.

"Harold, I truly do understand how difficult this is for you to agree to marry Ealdgyth. But Edith is an educated, intelligent woman. No one knows better than her that she cannot be your queen. She is the mother of your children, she will always be part of your life, even if you are King. Ealdgyth is a choice that will be accepted by the other earls as Queen and the North will be in accord with the rest of the country."

"Leofwine, I know the relationship between Edith and me will survive taking Ealdgyth as Queen. I'm not as concerned with that as I am with having taken that oath of fealty to William.. But the oath was taken on Holy relics. It was an oath before God! If William makes a claim for my loyalty, what can I do? England needs me right now, I can't just abandon my responsibilities and duty to my country!

"Harold, all you can do is deal with the here and now. Edward is dying and England will need a new King. And while you are the obvious choice, Edward has said nothing yet regarding his choice of heir and the Witenagemot has not met. What William will do, if anything, once a choice is made, hasn't happened yet."

Harold had no rejoinder to his brother's observation so remained silent, leaving his inner turmoil and self-doubts concerning the rightness of this decision and its complications to another day.

The following day, there continued to be reports of the King's condition. He was awake, albeit if only for a short period before he was again unresponsive. It was a common sight to walk around a corner and come upon a couple of men furtively discussing something; would the King die? When? Who would succeed him?

That night, while I was straightening Harold's chamber, he was summoned to King Edward's bedside. The King had briefly regained consciousness. No one objected when I slipped into the room behind Harold.

My aunt Edith was seated beside Edward's bed, nearly at his feet, the picture of piety and concern. However, I saw the look she directed at Harold as he entered. Though quickly masked, any expression of sisterly love was conspicuous by its absence!

I had been home long enough to realize that looks could be deceiving, particularly in the case of Edith Godwinesdatter.. After all, she was a Godwine She had grown up fending for herself in a family of six unruly, strong-willed boys. She was an educated, determined woman in a position of power which she didn't hesitate to use.

She had been the primary caretaker of the young Edgar since his father had died so shortly after arriving in England. She had made him a part of the royal household and urged

Edward to bestow the title Aetheling on him. In short, she had long ago determined that if she raised Edgar properly, she would be the power behind the throne when Edgar sat upon it.

One of the churchmen was supporting Edward in a semi-reclining position. His confessor was at his side. Edwin looked pretty awful, except for his eyes. At this time, they were bright with awareness and purpose. They conveyed that he knew he was dying, but was looking forward to meeting his God. It was hard to believe that just a month ago he had been hunting with Harold at Bosham.

Edward first spoke in praise of his wife, Edith, for her *dutiful and loving service.* Edith, sitting there, modestly lowered her eyes. If he only knew what I really thought of him, he wouldn't be saying that, thought Edith. If it hadn't been for the chance to bear him an heir after he let Archbishop Robert send me to a nunnery, he would have met his Maker long ago. When that didn't happen, at least he listened to Harold and me and let Archbishop Ealdred go looking for Edward the Exile in Hungary.

Then, having spoken so lovingly of his wife and in the presence of his wife, many of his earls, including Harold and Mocar, his confessor and his doctors, King Edward delivered his bombshell. Pointing to Earl Harold of Wessex, he declared, "I commend this woman and all the kingdom to your protection. Serve and honor her [[Edith] with faithful obedience as your lady and sister, which she is, and do not despoil her as long as she lives, of any honor got from me. Likewise, I commend those men who have left their native land for love of me and have up till now served me faithfully. Take from them an oath of fealty, if they should so wish, and protect and retain them or send them with your safe conduct across the Channel to their own homes with all that they have acquired in my service."

There was a moment of stunned silence. No one particularly wanted Edgar the Aethling to become king, but all had more or less expected Edward to name him as his successor. After all, there were no other Aethelings to choose among.

King Edward, ignoring the sudden and complete silence his words had caused, consoled Edith who had begun softly weeping in a show of grief for her departing husband but more likely in dismay that she was not to be even a co-regent.

He continued on, giving instructions for his burial in his newly consecrated Westminster Abbey and, finally, giving up the struggle, died.

The King's dying declaration solved the problem of the succession. There was no greater or more obligatory oath or command than a dying declaration. Irrespective of what Edward might have said or implied years earlier, and notwithstanding his apparent aim to be succeeded by Edgar the Aetheling, King Edward had made Harold his heir and given the kingdom into his keeping.

Harold looked stunned by the King's last words. He knew it was the right decision but had not truly expected Edward to make it. As he and the other earls and prelates filed out of the chamber still somewhat in shock, it took several moments of confusion before Harold awoke to the fact that they were looking to him to decide what to do next.

Gathering his wits about him, Harold turned to the others. "First thing in the morning, there must be a gathering of the Witenagemot in the King's council chambers. I will see you all there at the conclusion of Mass."

As the most powerful Earl among them, Harold opened the assembly, saying, "By now, you have all have heard that he last words of King Edward gave the kingdom into my keeping. You also know that there is an Atheling of the royal Saxon line of Alfred, who has a blood claim to the throne. King Harald Hardrada of Norway is also claiming rights to the throne from former King Canute. Last, but not least, although you may not as yet be aware, William the Bastard, Duke of Normandy will likely claim Edward promised that he, William, was his heir.

"It is my opinion that it is likely that one or more of these men will attempt to impose their belief that they have a right to the throne by promise, or blood or by force in the near future. Whoever becomes King, the selection surely will be disputed by one or more of these men. To survive, England must be united in its leadership. Each and all of these matters must be considered carefully. England's survival may depend upon it."

Striding to the door, Harold turned and added, "As the heir named by King Edward, I will not be present during your deliberations."

Once outside the chamber, he took a deep breath and said a fervent prayer for England's future. He recounted the votes of the earls and prelates who had approached him and combined with the northern votes, was certain the Witan would support King Edward's declaration. While still deeply conflicted about the effect his oath to William might have, he was certain that accepting the throne was the only way to see England through these troubled times.

Upon Harold's exit, Archbishop Ealdred of York turned to the assembled leaders of the realm who comprised the Witenagemot. "Is there any further discussion to be had about the successor to our late King, Edward? Many of us were present to hear for ourselves King Edward's final words naming Harold as his heir. Morcar, Edwin, will the North accept Harold as king?"

Morcar answered for both of them. "We have met with Harold and are agreed it is in the best interests of the country for Harold to be confirmed as Edward's heir. The Atheling is too young and untried to take the throne in these troubled times.

Leofwine spoke up. "I believe I speak for all of us when I say we are united that a foreigner must not become king. We all know of Harold's qualities. Granted he is my brother and I naturally support him, but we are all aware of his ability to govern England. He has effectively been doing so for the past several years, with Edward's blessing.

"Then, if there is nothing further to discuss and we are in agreement, Leofwine, please call Harold to return to hear our decision," Archbishop Ealdred said.

The following day, after the funeral and internment of Kind Edward, Ealdred, Archbishop of York, as the leading prelate of the realm crowned and anointed Harold as King Harold II. Although traditionally the Archbishop of Canterbury would be the highest ranking prelate in the land, and therefore be the one to anoint a new king, Harold and the Witan asked Ealdred to perform the consecration. The See of Canterbury, and who was its legitimate archbishop, was still a matter of contention as a result of the outlawing of Robert of Jumièges, the previously appointed Archbishop. Edward's appointment of Stigand in his place while Robert still lived was challenged by the Church as against church rules and policy. At the conclusion of the consecration, in accordance with the customs and laws of England, the leading earls, prelates and thegns of the kingdom pledged the traditional oaths of loyalty and submission to him as he, in turn, pledged to govern justly and in accordance with the laws of the kingdom.

The English magnates were satisfied with the resolution of the succession issue. It was now up to Harold II Rex to deal with the other claimants to the throne of England, who certainly would not be as willing as the English to accept the choice of Edward and the Witenagemot.

January 15th, 1066
Conches en Ouche, Normandy

Our household had just finished hearing Mass. We were about to sit at the high table to break the night's fast when the commotion of a rider galloping into the bailey drew everyone's attention.

The house guard brought the rider to the me, recognizing the colors of the rider as those of William, Duke of Normandy. I opened the message and read its contents. It was an urgent summons from the Duke as vassal and friend, to attend Duke William at Falaise. Rising from the table, I issued orders as I left the hall to oversee the gathering of supplies and equipment for travel.

"Bailiff, see that my horse is ready to travel within the hour. Squire, get this messenger some food and drink and a new horse. Sergeant, see to it that an escort troop is ready to ride within the hour. Each man is to have an extra horse as well as ones for me and the courier. Turning to my wife, I asked, "Would you see that food is prepared to take with us, since I have yet to eat and it will be a long, hard ride."

Within a short time, all of us were galloping on the road to Falaise.

During a rest break and change to the relief horses, I had a chance, at last, to speak with the messenger. "What is this all about? Do you know?"

"I don't really know, my Lord. All I know is that a courier who had been traveling hard, arrived, I think from England,

and was taken to the Duke. There was some shouting, and then I was summoned and ordered to come get you as quickly as possible.

It was dark by the time we arrived at Falaise the following day. We were tired and dirty but nonetheless, I was escorted without delay to the Duke."

He was awaiting us as the outriders had informed him of our arrival. He strode back and forth, wearing a path, if that were possible, in the stone floor of his business chamber, muttering invectives. In such a tall man, his anger was truly intimidating. A timid messenger was partially obscured by the shadows of the room. As the bearer of bad news, and the cause of William's wrath, he was attempting to remain as invisible and out of the path of the ducal temper as possible. He was relieved at the entrance of someone else to attract the Duke's attentions. Knowing William's turbulent childhood and the many attempts to kill him or wrest control of the duchy from him, I understood how he had become a man famous for his vitriolic reactions when events did not fall in with his desires or goals. However, that did not make it any less dangerous to be around him at such a time.

Vos entered the chamber, still covered with road grime, and clearly weary from the fast pace maintained getting to Falaise. "William, what has happened that is so urgent?"

"If Edward were not already dead, I would kill him myself, the lying ingrate," William ranted. "After all the years he spent here in Normandy. After all we did for him! We sheltered him during his exile. We kept him safe so he could eventually claim his inheritance. We gave him a HOME! Edward recognized all this when he promised I would be his heir and successor! Such a promise can't be undone. Now, on his deathbed, did he keep this promise? No. He declared Harold Godwineson his heir!" William gestured to the cringing messenger, ordering. "Tell him."

The messenger said he had just arrived from England, and recounted the events which had taken place in England, particularly Edward's dying declaration giving the kingdom, his wife and vassals into the care of Harold Godwineson, Earl of Wessex.

The messenger added that a witenagemot was present. since all the leading magnates of England were already at Westminster for the Christmas festivities and the consecration of Edward's new cathedral. It had met the morning after Edward's death. At the meeting these leading earls, prelate and influential thegns of England had confirmed their support of Edward's nomination of Harold as his successor. The day of Edward's burial, the Archbishop of York anointed Harold and he was crowned King.

Upon receiving his crown and scepter, Harold then took the traditional oath of loyalty from the leading earls, prelates and thegns of the kingdom and, in turn, gave his pledge to them to rule in accordance with custom and law.

Sending the courier away, William exploded, "Edward breaking his promise to me is bad enough, Vos, but that oath-breaker Harold! He took an oath on holy relics to support me. He swore allegiance to me! It is his duty to support his liege lord and his liege lord was promised the throne of England. It is his DUTY to support my right to England's throne! Instead, he has taken the crown for himself! Harold is an oath-breaker, a perjurer! Harold is foresworn; he has usurped the crown from me. I am the rightful King of England and I'll take the throne by force, if necessary. The throne of England is mine!"

Richard Vos had his hands full attempting to calm William. Efforts to reason with William in one of his rages were not usually very successful, but I had to try. "William, please, calm down; think about this. You're talking about a war. A war with a country that is three times as big as Normandy, and is on the other side of a sizable body of water with dangerous currents and winds—you're not talking about just a quick hit and run raid. If I understand what you are saying, you are proposing to invade England with an army and conquer it!"

William curtailed his angry striding to stand virtually towering over me. He looked down, his brown eyes almost black with his venom. "This will not go unaddressed, Richard. Harold is a usurper, an oath-breaker, and I will not allow him to take what is rightfully mine. I will do whatever it takes to see that he pays for this."

"William, listen to reason. Not only is an invasion of England not a very practical undertaking, but it's expensive and will take time. Normandy has no standing army. You can't order your vassals to fight for you outside of France, so who would make up this invading force? Where would the ships to ferry this force across the Channel come from? There must be other ways to resolve this," Vos pleaded. "What about the newly formed Association of International Communities? We could bring this matter before the AIC. They have the power to remedy this situation. Let them bring pressure on England to acknowledge your rights in the matter."

"Vos, that will take too long, and in the meantime, who knows what actions Harold will take as king? Something must be done right now," replied William, but at last calming enough to sit and drink from his goblet.

"Such an application and the subsequent proceedings won't take as long as it would to build a fleet of ships to transport an army you don't have, across the Channel to England," I replied.

"You can start the process by putting this matter before the AIC right now! You can assert your claim and all the international communities will know about it. Harold can't just ignore your claim as if it didn't exist, if it's brought before the AIC."

"What if Harold won't go to before the Association?"

"Well, you always have your first option available—to invade—and it will certainly look better to the international community that you tried to resolve the matter without a war. In addition, if he ignores the AIC and refuses to participate in any resolution, the Association can take action and impose sanctions. Then he has isolated England from all the international communities. I can't see him taking that risk. If, on the other hand, Harold admits to the jurisdiction of the Association, he will then have to abide by their decision, even if their judgment is against him. If he doesn't, he will be proven to have been twice foresworn. No one will owe him any political, moral or religious allegiance.

"As a practical matter, although we would have to first place our claim before the Executive Council of the AIC, where it would be debated as to whether the claim should be placed before the entire body, I don't think the Council will do that. It is far more likely they will sidestep the whole issue and send it on to the High Court for the AIC to handle. After all, who is the legitimate king is primarily a legal issue. If the AIC Council does this, then there would be a trial with a panel of international judges to hear the matter, and each party would present its arguments by the testimony of their witnesses."

William, his brow furrowed in thought, stood suddenly and paced again. "You speak of having witnesses appear in court. What if we produce a witness who could say the Pope supports my right to be King, agreeing that Harold is forsworn and is owed no allegiance by his subjects?" he queried.

"I think that would be a powerful witness for your claims and carry a lot of weight with the justices of the court. But after your long battle with the Pope when he forbade your marriage to Matilda, would he be likely to side with you in this matter?" I asked.

"I think he might. He wants reform of the Church in England. Matilda and I did our penance. We founded the two churches as directed. Relations have been cordial the past several years, and the Church would have a lot to gain if I win. I need to talk to Abbot Lanfranc about this. He is too old to travel to Rome himself, so we need to figure out who could be sent to argue our case to gain the papal support. Who do you think could be a strong advocate?"

"Well, the first thought that comes to mind is your half-brother Bishop Odo, but as I think about it, his reputation isn't very *priestly*. Someone whose reputation as a churchman is above reproach would be a better ambassador. Let me think about it," I replied. "In the meantime, I'll get started on a Request for Resolution to place the matter before the AIC Council."

"While you're doing that, I will send my own message to Harold. I'll remind him of his promise to support my lawful claim upon Edward's death. Remind him that the promise was sworn on holy relics and he is bound by that oath in the eyes of God. He will find out soon enough that we are seeking enforcement of my rights in the AIC's Council and/or Court." Turning to one of his men-at-arms, he barked, "Get that messenger in here right now."

Upon the courier's reluctant return, William ordered, "Take this exact message to Earl Harold. Tell him 'You will have nothing to fear from me and can live the rest of your life secure if, within the space of one year, you have not seen me in the place where you think your feet are safest'. Now go!"

After first repeating the exact message to be sure he had it correctly, the courier escaped the Duke's presence to return to England.

After the courier left, William said, "I must leave for Lillebonne in a few days, Richard—to hold a court session and deal with some other matters. Since I would go through Caen anyway, I can also stop to see Abbot Lanfranc to discuss the situation with him. I expect to be back here in a fortnight or so. By that time, you should have a draft of the Request to the Council ready. We can review it then and agree on a final copy."

When we met two days later, I reported to William the information I'd discovered: I had spent the last forty-eight hours gathering information to brief William on what would be the procedure regarding the Request be heard by the Council and if necessary, an Application to the court, what procedures needed to be observed and specifically, what needed to be done first, and what kind of an outcome could be expected. In particular, I tried to impress upon him the fact that if the Council referred the matter to the High Court, by going before the Court, there would be a trial during which both sides would have the opportunity to present testimony by witnesses. William would have the opportunity to present the rightness of his claim to an audience of his world-wide peers.

William thought about these points for a few minutes while he paced the confines of the chamber. Stopping before the window leaking the chill January air into the room, he turned and asked, "But what if the Council or Court decides against me? Then what? Do I have to accept it?"

"In theory, yes. By going before the AIC you agree to its jurisdiction to resolve the matter and to abide by its decision. In practice, who can say? You still remain Duke of Normandy. Any court action has no effect on that. As Duke, you make decisions regarding Normandy's best interests as you always have. Only you can decide whether you want to pursue your claim to the throne, even if it means going against a decision of your neighboring sovereignties."

We were interrupted by the appearance of William's bailiff at the chamber door, seeking William's immediate attention to an urgent matter which had arisen. Dismissing me, the Duke said, "I'll think about this and tomorrow, after chapel, we'll discuss whether to proceed further with this. Then I must leave for Lillebonne."

As I said my evening prayers before retiring that night, I included one that William would be led to decide to put the problem before the Court, even though it went against the grain of his character.

The following morning, while the clerks started on the formal parts of the Request for Resolution, William and I strategized how best to present the arguments of his claim. The Request needed to be as succinct and forceful as possible.

William was adamant that its main thrust be that Edward had promised he was his heir and that the promise was irrevocable.

"The designation of someone as heir can't be revoked, Vos. It's a *post obitum* gift. Once made, it stands. It is irrevocable. I am the heir to King Edward."

"That may be true, William, but the problem is that there is no one today who can substantiate that such a promise was ever made or the terms of the promise. Archbishop Robert of Jumièges has been dead for ten years. Edward is dead. All the English magnates whom Archbishop Robert said constituted a witengemot and swore to support you as heir are no longer available to testify. Godwine and the former northern earls of Northumbria and Mercia are dead and have been succeeded by their sons, who swore no such allegiance.

"On the other hand, many of your comtes and vassals saw Harold swear fealty to you on holy relics. They might not know the exact words that he spoke but they saw him take a solemn oath on relics and an altar to you as his overlord. To fail to support you, his liege lord, now makes him an oath-breaker. The members of the Council are unlikely to have much sympathy or understanding for someone like that."

"I know what I was promised! My testimony that Edward made such a promise will have to be enough. Include both reasons, the promise and Harold's oath, as grounds, as well as anything else you can think of, in the Request."

Then, in his usual decisive and calculating manner, he said, "Richard, proceed with whatever is necessary to place this before the Council of the Association of International Communities (AIC) or even its Court. Get this started as quickly as possible. I want no delays. Harold needs to be prevented from establishing his claim and challenged as soon as possible."

January 20th, 1066
Falaise, Normandy

I left William pleased that a plan was taking form and that he seemed ready to apply his well-honed strategic skills to the endeavor, even if not wildly enthusiastic about going to the AIC Council or court instead of battle. I was sure that placing the matter before the Association of International Communities was the better way to deal with the situation but I was still surprised William was persuaded to do so, and to abandon his initial response to invade England. Had he really given up all intention to do so? I wasn't convinced but I had done everything I could to avoid such an action. So, ignoring my reservations, for the next several days I made good use of a cadre of clerks—available as a result of William's and his wife Matilda's generosity to the Church—to draft the documents required to make the formal Request for Resolution to the AIC Council and, just in case, the Application for hearing by the Court.

Upon completion of the drafted documents, I read them to William for his approval before he left for Lillebonne. He had not volunteered the reason for going to Lillebonne, and I had not asked. I was later to wish I had.

I sent the Request to the Council to be filed with the Secretary of the Association of International Communities at Ghent. As I had read the documents to William, the thought crossed my mind that it was a good thing I was loyal to William. I could have put almost anything in the written documents and he would not have known of it until it was too late to do anything about it. It never ceased to amaze me how such a charismatic leader never bothered to learn to read or write. How did he expect to rule a county so much larger than Normandy? Normandy was only slightly bigger than Harold's lands of Wessex, and that was only a portion of England!

The Request had set forth William's grounds for disputing the coronation of Harold. (1) That it was invalid because Edward's prior designation of William as his heir, was a post obitum gift and as such was irrevocable; (2) in accordance with the irrevocability of a *post obitum* gift of the succession to the throne, upon King Edward's death, the life estate as king he had reserved to himself was extinguished and William immediately had the right to exercise the powers of the office as king; (3) that Harold had taken a solemn oath on Holy relics that he would support William's claim to the throne, which he had not kept, with the result he was an oath-breaker; and (4) as an oath-breaker, he was not eligible to be king.

In conclusion, William requested the coronation of Harold be declared invalid—null and void—that Harold be set aside as king; and finally, that William be declared the rightful king of England.

January 27th, 1066
Bosham, England

Harold relaxed from the hectic first month of kingship, with a quick trip to Bosham to visit with his children and the love of his life Edith (known as *Swanneck*, a poor translation of her name in English but also for her lovely feature). As usual, I accompanied Harold.

He was telling Edith of the initial message from William. Harold, ordinarily a man slow to anger, raised his voice as his temper increased just in the retelling of the message. "That arrogant bastard! Who does he think he is threatening England? Threatening me!" Harold sputtered.

"Calm down, Harold. For all you know William is just being William—lash out at anyone or anything that displeases him. You know his temper—you saw it often enough while you were there."

"I know, I know," replied Harold, ceasing his pacing and taking a seat. "But I know him well enough to know that he is going to do something about my becoming king. I just don't know what. Enough of that! What I really need to discuss with you and the children are the changes that will come upon my impending church marriage to Ealdgyth of Northumbria. Edith, you know that as little as possible will change. You are the mother of my children and my love. But England needs a queen and legitimate heirs. As King, I can do no less."

They were interrupted by the commotion of the arrival of a messenger who was escorted to Harold. He handed Harold an official looking message.

After reading the message, Harold handed it to Edith. He said, "Edith, read this," while calling to the children, "Alright, outside now, I need to talk to your mother."

Edith read the message, and then showed it to me. Edith turned to Harold. "Well, this is a surprise! But at least you now know what is he planning to do. What does this mean, Harold?"

"It means that William won't take my being King without a fight." Harold gathered his things for an early return to London. He stopped long enough to add, "I was expecting some reaction from him, but I thought it might be more on the order of an invasion, not this Request for Resolution to the AIC. Though I must admit, I would rather respond to a petition than a fleet of warships. I have to get back to London, my love. I'm sorry we have had so little time together. This Request must be answered as soon as possible. Leofwine and I, as well as some others, must determine the best way to respond to it. I also need to see if I can find out if this is the only action that William is going to take. Harkon, will you call one of the couriers? Send him to find Leofwine—ask him to meet me at Westminster as soon as he can. We should be there by Monday evening at the latest." Harold finalized his preparations to leave, said goodbye to the children and Edith, and we were quickly on our way to London.

After Harold left, and she had gotten the children settled down, Edith sat with her embroidery reflecting on the day's news. *William's willingness to do battle over the kingship could be dangerous not only to Harold but also to our children*, she thought. *If something were to happen to Harold, it would be completely up to me to protect them. Everything Harold has ever said about William shows how ruthless he can be when it suits him. Now that Harold has a wife, would William consider my children a threat to him, even if Harold were captured or even dead? Or would he think of them as illegitimate as he was, and have some sympathy for them? Do I dare plan on his being sympathetic? I could move to one of my more remote holdings; maybe out of sight would be out of mind. But Harold needs me now as never before. I can't just go away and deprive him of my support and his children now when he needs us most. But, she decided, I could make the holdings at Walsingham ready in case we had to retreat there.* At least that much could be done.

With her mind somewhat more at ease, Edith settled into the embroidery task before her, running through in her mind the actions to be taken to ready Walsingham.

January 30th,1066
London, England

Leofwine was waiting in King Harold's quarters at Westminster when Harold and I arrived, travel-stained and weary. Harold handed Leofwine a rolled message tube.

"Read this, while I wash off some of the road dust and get something to drink. I'm glad you were able to get here so quickly."

"I was already in London when the messenger found me," said Leofwine. "What is this—when did it come?"

"It was delivered to me at Bosham. I started back for London as soon as I could. I'm not sure what the procedures of the AIC are but we better find out."

"I was surprised," said Harkon to Leofwine. "Oh, not that William would make an objection to Harold's crowning, but that he would go to the AIC. That isn't his way to do things. At least not that I saw in the twelve years I was his hostage. I would almost expect him to be here personally, ranting and raging on your doorstep."

"I suspect you are right," Harold replied. "I think we have to be prepared for more than just a Request to the AIC Council. The question is, what else will he do? But, first things first. We need to learn the procedures regarding a Request for Resolution to the AIC Council and figure out what, if anything, the Council is likely to do with such a request. Leofwine, will you work on it and meet with me in a day or so to discuss what must be done? If a response is required, the point has to be strongly made that the Council doesn't have the right or the power to remove an anointed king. In addition, the Council has no jurisdiction to interfere with the peaceful, legitimate, internal procedures for the succession of a country's leader. But the proper time and means to assert this must be determined. In the meantime, I will have to speak with some of the other Witan members about this development."

January 30th, 1066
Lillebonne, Normandy

At his huge, rambling castle overlooking the river Seine's entry to the sea, William of Normandy awaited the arrival of his nobles and neighboring dukes and counts for a conference. He thought about his decision to deliberately withhold the information from Vos about the meeting, especially since he had agreed Vos should go forward with the Request to the AIC. *No,* he said to himself, *he doesn't need to know, at least not for now. I'm not willing to limit my options in this battle. Calling for this conference has no bearing on any petition Vos would draft.*

William paced the room as he anxiously awaited the gathering of these men. His thoughts focused on the meeting. *This has to happen! It is imperative these men are persuaded an invasion of England is possible and worthwhile. Somehow I must convince them that not only will it be morally right, but it will be economically advantageous for them to support me in this.*

He knew he could not order his neighbors—hopefully future allies—to support him. Nor did his Norman nobles have any obligation to provide him service outside of Normandy. To gain their support and cooperation, they must be convinced an invasion would succeed and be profitable for all involved.

His bailiff announced that everyone had finally arrived. Proceeding to the chamber where his invitees were gathered,

William addressed them. "Friends, allies, I have asked you here to obtain your support and help in deposing the usurper Earl Harold of Wessex from the English throne. Many of you were present when he swore his oath of fealty to me on holy relics, his oath to support all my endeavors, including my claim to the English throne as Edward's designated heir. He swore to uphold my causes. Our own Archbishop Robert of Jumièges had personally delivered King Edward's words to me. Now that King Edward has died, it was Harold's sworn duty to support and acknowledge that I was king. Has he done that? No! Despite an oath to God, he has usurped the throne and made himself king. He has trampled on that sacred oath of fealty and is foresworn. He is not worthy to be king, having broken an oath before God.

There was an immediate uproar from the assembled men. They were not particularly concerned with the attempt at the moral high ground of William's rhetoric but with more practical matters. Various cries of, "It's not possible", "It can't be done", "England is too strong", "Where would we get enough ships to do such a thing?", "Who would pay for such a venture?" resounded in the hall. Given such an overwhelming negative reception to his plea, William quickly realized that he would have to alter his approach to the issue if there was to be any hope of success.

That evening, he sought out his half-brothers, Bishop Odo and Robert of Mortain. "Odo, Robert, I have to admit that did not go well today. We need these men! They must be convinced to join me. We have to approach them differently if there is to be any hope of success. Any suggestions?"

Odo replied after a few moments thought, "I think if you talk to them in small groups or even individually, they can be kept from ganging up on you. If I pledge the support of a hundred ships and all the fighting men such ships would hold, you could use that to solicit similar contributions from the others."

"And you could let it be known that I have pledged another one hundred twenty ships and fighting men to fill them," added Robert. "While our combined ships and men aren't enough, they certainly are enough to be the core of a sizable invasion force. An armada of that size should give your allies pause that it would be better to be with you than against you, to be sure these ships and men didn't descend upon them."

"I appreciate your support, my brothers. I think that meeting with each of the men separately is the thing to do. Letting them know there are already sizable pledges of men and ships should encourage each of the others to join in and be part of the enterprise. Many of these men have younger sons who are anxious for land and to make a name for themselves. But there is no hope of having land here in Normandy. England presents a tremendous opportunity for their futures."

February 10th, 1066
Reading, England

The courier from the AIC caught up with the court at Reading while it was on its progression back to Westminster. Harold, realizing the courier was from the AIC, sent for Leofwine. As his brother entered the chamber, Harold tossed the scroll to him. "Here, read this."

Leofwine deftly caught the scroll and read it. The Executive Council of the AIC had passed a Resolution. They had declined to debate the matter in the general meeting of the AIC. Considering the issue to be a legal matter, the Council had referred the matter to the High Court of the AIC. for hearing and determination.

"Well," Leofwine commented, "I would say that William is now stuck with having to go before the AIC Court, or ignore what he started, and go with what was probably his plan all along: use force to overthrow you. Can he find enough ships and men to mount a successful invasion, and would the international community support him if he goes to war? Crossing the Channel is a tricky business in the best of circumstances, as you know. Look what happened to you in '64 when you ended up as William's *guest.*

"The more I think about it, the more I think that this decision is a good one for us," Leofwine continued. "It gives us a much better forum to show that William has no legitimate claim. He's will have to present some sort of a credible case, first in a complaint setting forth legal reasoning for his claims and then produce witnesses and tangible proof to establish his claim. Not just scream loud and long from the rooftops that he has been wronged and expect to be believed. And all of this in accordance with the Court's timetable, deadlines and rules of court!

"William's Application to the Court for it to hear the case will probably be pretty much the same allegations as those he claimed when he asked the Executive Council to resolve the matter. As a matter of form," continued Leofwine, "we have to object to the Court hearing the dispute but it would really only be to protect our position. We are members of the AIC so have already admitted to the Court's right to accept application for hearing. Once William's Application for Hearing has been accepted and our objection to it and our allegations that the Court lacks jurisdiction over the matter have been filed and duly noted, William will have to file his Complaint in accordance with a schedule ordered by the Court."

"What if I refuse to participate because I don't agree to the court's jurisdiction to hear the matter?" asked Harold. "Particularly as to their jurisdiction to rule on the issue of being a legally anointed king."

"Typically, the Court could claim that you were properly served, and that as a member of the Association of International Communities, you have already accepted their jurisdiction to hear disputes between members. It likely would default you and decide in William's favor. It could also impose sanctions against England to enforce its decision. Even if the other international communities didn't really believe in the truth of the claims, they would have a lot of economic reasons to go along with it and garner to themselves a share of the trade now benefiting England.

"However, that isn't to say that the jurisdiction of the Court to determine the validity of a country's procedures to determine the successive ruler upon the death of the prior ruler can't be challenged as beyond the founding charter grant of jurisdiction to the Court. It would be a strategic decision as well as a procedural one as to when would be the proper and best way to raise that question."

Turning to Leofwine, Harold, shrugged. "Well, we have to be prepared to vigorously defend our country, both on paper and militarily. I certainly don't trust William to give up any idea of military force to back up his claim, even though he has gone to the Court. Knowing William as I do to my sorrow, he is unlikely to rely on only one plan of attack." Still mentally wresting with his personal demons, Harold continued, "What do you think will happen when the earls find out about my oath to William? So far, only a few Englishmen know of it. Edward knew. I told him about it as soon as I returned from Normandy. Obviously, he didn't give much credence to it. He allowed me to witness sworn documents afterwards, so he clearly didn't consider me foresworn-but what of the others? Will they understand that I had to take the damn oath to save the lives of my hostage brother and nephew and my men?"

"I don't think the Witan will desert you," replied Leofwine. "0Most importantly, they don't want William, a bastard and a foreigner on the throne. Anyone would be better than that. It's possible that they could consider Harald Hardrada of Norway, but not likely. The North is more English than Scandinavian now. I doubt that anyone wants a Norwegian king as our king. We both know that an oath on relics is important, but it wouldn't be the first time an oath of fealty was repudiated."

"If only I hadn't been so unaware of William's real intent," Harold said. "I shouldn't have allowed myself to get into that situation! It's like the tale of the fox and the crow and I'm the stupid crow! I still can see myself standing there with one hand on an altar and the other on a covered casket taking that Oath of fealty. And I didn't even think about what might be in the covered casket! At least I didn't pay homage to him. The oath was bad enough."

Harold, pacing and frowning, continued, "What about the justices of the AIC court? What do you suppose will be their reaction once they learn about the oath? William will be certain they know of it. That's one of his main arguments. Will they believe that I broke a promise to God?"

"Harold, I can't say with any certainty, but remember, they are all leaders of their people. I'm certain that when this matter goes to trial, we can convince them that *'there but for the Grace of God go I'*; that more is at stake here than giving in to William's schemes and what he would have them believe."

"Let's deal with today's problems for now and deal with tomorrow's when they arrive," replied Harold. "Will you see to it that messengers are sent to as many prelates and earls and thegns as possible to come to Westminster for a meeting of the Witenagemot? Most of them will be here for the Easter Festival but that isn't until mid-April and we can't wait that long. They need to know what is happening now, and I need to know their thoughts on the matter so we can decide how we are going to deal with it!"

After Leofwine left, Harold paced and thought about what he would say to the men of the Witenagemot when they met. He debated his actions in the past. He thought he had acted as a king should act in the face of William's actions but even knowing this to be true, it did little to assuage his emotional inner turmoil. How could he present a defense at a trial without perjuring himself? He had sworn that damn oath to William. If everyone didn't know of it now, they certainly would shortly. It was on holy relics—an oath to God. Did God really want him to support William's claim to the throne of England, as insubstantial and false as that claim was? Was he really bound to support William as his liege lord in this absurd endeavor? Could he be a part of delivering England to the sovereignty of a bastard, foreign duke?

As Harold pondered the present situation, his thoughts spun like a cat chasing its tail. He had more questions than answers. But if he couldn't gain the support of the Witan, how could he present a defense in a court of his peers? Whatever else William might do, he certainly would go forward with a complaint to the AIC's court. It was clear that there would be an open trial of these matters.

But the more he thought about how to present the situation to the Witan, the more he came to realize that William had a problem with his claim to be the named heir. In the face of the testimony of all the persons present at Edward's dying declaration, William would have to admit that it was Edward who was foresworn, if his alleged promise to William had been made and it was irrevocable. Edward would be the one to have breached his promise—if it was ever even made—to William by naming Harold. It was Edward who had made the promise and he was the one who, on his deathbed, declared something different. The more he thought about it, the more Harold came to realize that it was very unlikely that anyone would believe that the saintly King Edward, knowing he was dying, would place himself in a position whereby he would be foresworn. Certainly not on his deathbed, minutes away from meeting his God!

March 6th, 1066
Rouen, Normandy

While William was traveling the duchy, Richard Vos returned to his home in Conches en Ouche to work on polishing the final draft of the Complaint to the Court of the AIC. As the situation progressed, he felt as if it were taking on a life of its own and that no matter which way he turned, it looked like the end result would not be in favor of his Conches en Ouche holdings. He realized as he put together the legal Petition just how flimsy was the legal support for William's position. *If William lost the court decision, William will not be the only one to lose. I'll be lucky if I retain my title and lands to say nothing of my life.*

If William won the Court battle, how likely was it that England would accept the Court's decision? Vos had no trouble answering that question. "Not at all likely! Even if Harold stepped down, the people would surely revolt. That would mean battles and while William seemed to thrive on them, the days of my enjoying being a warrior have long passed. In battles, people are killed! Governing Conches suits me fine. But if William goes to war, so must I!"

Le Viconte de Conches en Ouches was saved from his gloomy introspection by the arrival of a messenger from William informing him that William would return to Rouen in three days, and that Gilbert of Lisieux would be arriving in Rouen at the same time. When William arrived, he would meet with both of them. Richard was glad that he was almost finished with the petition to court. He would have just enough time to finish it and get to Rouen.

Richard thought about the coming meeting with Archdeacon Gilbert as he made his way to the meeting. What did William have in mind? Trying to fathom the man's machinations could be a full time job! Not coming up with any answers to his own questions, Vos gave up the puzzle. Now that William was returning, he was about to find out what was or possibly would be Archdeacon Gilbert involvement in this matter.

March 9th, 1066
Rouen, Normandy

At William's residence at Rouen, Richard and Archdeacon Gilbert of Lisieux exchanged pleasantries while awaiting the arrival of Duke William. The archdeacon was trying to appear calm, but that was far from what he truly felt. It wasn't every day he was summoned to the duke, for a reason he had yet to discover. Vos offered him some wine and was attempting to put his at his ease, when William strode into the chamber.

"Ah, Father Gilbert! I hope you had an uneventful trip? Travel at this time of the year can be so unpredictable. However, you should encounter much more pleasant weather in the travel I have in mind for you."

Gilbert didn't know whether to be pleased or apprehensive. It hadn't occurred to him that as a result of the summons to attend the Duke, he would be sent on a journey.

William continued, "Vicomte Vos and I have previously discussed the value of sending an envoy to Pope Alexander II to enlist his support in a situation which has arisen. You may not know it, but Harold, Earl of Wessex, has usurped the throne of England, which was promised to me by the former king, Edward the Confessor. I must send an envoy to Rome to bring this matter to His Holiness's attention and enlist his aid and support to gain my rightful heritage. We will also be gong before the Association of International Communities High Court to pursue this issue. But in the meantime, Rome needs to become aware of the situation and lend its voice in support to my position. I think you would be an eminently suitable person to send to Rome to accomplish this."

Archdeacon Gilbert was speechless. He had no idea what would be a proper response to what William said. "Milord, I don't know what to say. You do me great honor, but are you sure that I am the one you should send to Rome?" he ventured at last. "I am only an archdeacon and not at all familiar with the cardinals of Rome, or the Pope."

"Yes, I believe you are," replied William. "You are a well-regarded churchman and an acknowledged scholar of cannon law. The Pope must be brought to understand that King Edward of England made a lawful *inter vivos* gift, a *post orbitum* grant of the lands and crown of England to me as his heir. As you well know, the effects of this type of gift are delayed until the death of the donor, at which point the donee comes into full possession and control of the gift previously given to him. In addition, the gift is irrevocable; the gift carries with it the renunciation on the donor's part of his right of revocation. Word has come that Edward named Harold as his heir on his deathbed, but he had no right to do so. His prior gift to me was irrevocable." William, his voice rising and hardening, continued, "Another part of the mission to Pope Alexander is to urge that he take action against Harold, personally excommunicate him, for instance. Harold is foresworn of his oath of fealty to me and he has forfeited any rights he may have had to be king. Even if he was named by Edward, he was prevented from accepting Edward's nomination by his oath to be my liegeman and support my causes."

William rose and strode to the sideboard, refilling his wine goblet with a trembling hand as he strove to curb his temper that the mere discussion of Harold's transgressions was causing to surface. Taking his time, with his back to Vos and Gilbert, he said, "Vos, is there anything else Gilbert should put before His Holiness?"

"I would suggest the reformation of the Church in England would be an issue that would certainly be within the jurisdiction of the Pope to address. Look at the situation with Stigand. Is he an archbishop or not? I think it can be justly argued that the state of the English Church is in dire straits if a foresworn person is allowed to remain as its king. The Pope needs to be persuaded that this would be the perfect opportunity for him to do something about it," replied Vos.

"Father Gilbert, Abbot Lanfranc has prepared some documents setting forth some points of the arguments to be made, in order to aid you in this mission," added William. "Richard, escort Gilbert to see that he has all of this information ready to take with him and prepare any other papers to the Pope. I will sign them when they are ready. Gilbert, make your arrangements to leave as soon as possible, certainly within the week. Let me know when that will be. After you get Gilbert settled, Richard, return and we will go over the court documents to be filed."

As Vos and Gilbert left the chamber, William sat back with a satisfied grin, thinking, *One more arrow shot to the heart of Harold.*

Vos, after he had settled Gilbert with the various documents for his journey, rejoined William with the drafted court documents in hand.

"From the size of that bundle of documents, it looks like you were busy while I was away," quipped William.

"There are numerous formalities to be observed, but I believe these draft documents are in accordance with the court rules," replied Vos, oblivious to William's attempt at good humor.

Well, tell me what we are asking of the Court. Just the short version, I don't need to hear all the flowery nonsense that the legal system so enjoys," William responded.

Starting at the top of his stack of documents, Vos, all serious, explained. "First there is our ambassador at Ghent's letter to the Court's Registrar telling the court that I am Normandy's agent. Then there's a letter from me on your behalf stating in general the substance of our claim. Those documents were sent to the court as our Application to be heard by the Court, which you have already approved. Next is the Order from the court accepting the case to be heard by the Justices of the Court and setting forth the initial timetable. The Plaintiff's complaint is due by March 27th and England's answer to your complaint is due by April 17th.

"The first part of the Complaint is mainly an explanation of who the parties are, that the Court has jurisdiction, and the background facts which have led up to Harold being crowned. The actual counts of the Complaint are the important parts. I have alleged three counts: the first of Fraud; Harold took an oath to you, with no intent to perform its duties, and didn't keep to his obligations. The second count of Undue Influence alleges that by undue influence, due to his trusted position and his power, Harold wrongfully persuaded Edward to name him his heir, thereby breaking his irrevocable promise to you, and preventing you from becoming king. Then there is a third court alleging that Edward granted you an irrevocable *post obitum* gift of the lands of England as its king and therefore, his life estate being terminated, you immediately have all the rights and privileges of the gift."

"If the Pope is persuaded to support me, can something be added to the pleading that would let the Court know of his support?" asked William.

"By the time we have heard from the Pope it would likely be too late to be allowed to add a new cause of action.

However, we could have Gilbert as a witness and get the testimony before the court in that way," answered Vos.

"Thinking about the background information of the Complaint, did you include all the years we supported Edward and provided him and his brother with a home? The Court has to know that Edward owed us, that that was one of the reasons why he made me his heir."

"Yes, I specifically mentioned in the background information that for nearly two thirds of Edward's life, he had been sheltered, supported, and raised in Normandy."

"Good. And the relationship with my Great Aunt Matilda, King Edward's mother?"

"Yes that is included."

"Go ahead and file the papers now. I appreciate that you have these documents ready to be filed earlier than the due date. This matter needs to be kept on as tight a schedule as we can make happen. Delay is an advantage to Harold."

Upon receipt of the documents from Richard Vos, William's ambassador at Ghent prepared and transmitted to the Court, the formal Complaint of Duke William of Normandy for the Court's consideration with a copy sent to Harold's chancellor in England.

March 13th,1066
London, England

Leofwine entered Harold's chamber, documents in hand.

"You're dripping water all over my chamber, Leofwine,!"

"Sorry, Harold, but its pouring out there and I was trying to keep these messages which just arrived, dry. Leofwine dug under his wet cloak for the papers and handed them to Harold. "You need to see these."

Harold first noticed the seal of the AIC Court on its order, then realized that the documents were the acceptance by the Court to hear the matter, the Court's initial due dates for pleadings and from Vicomte Vos, a copy of William's Complaint filed with the Court.

"Well, he's finally done it. He's going to court. But what about our spy's report of the meeting in Lillebonne? Was that meeting just to sound things out as insurance or is he playing his usual game of duplicity and getting prepared to invade in case the court rules against him?" asked Harold.

"Hard to say," replied Leofwine. "Knowing how ruthless he can be I would suspect he wants to be prepared in case he doesn't like the court's decision. But, at least any invasion would probably be delayed until the court renders a decision. And if the case lasts, or the decision isn't reached until winter, then any invasion wouldn't be until next spring."

Harold handed Leofwine a goblet of wine as he stood before the fire trying to dry off. "After we respond to this Complaint, what comes next?"

"According to the Order which was included, William's complaint wasn't due until March 20th, even though it was filed on the13th of March. We have until the 17th of April to file our Answer."

Harold thought about what Leofwine said. Joining Leofwine before the warmth of the fire, he shared his thinking and strategizing with his brother. "Certainly, we must respond to the Complaint. Particularly any supposed right of the Court to depose an anointed king needs to be challenged. Since we are a member of the AIC, I suppose that we have to agree that the Court has the right to at least listen to Normandy's arguments. But that still doesn't mean they can remove a sovereign."

"Now that the Complaint has been received, I think it would be wise to review it with the witan. There should be enough time to do so and respond with our answer by the deadline.It is to our advantage to use all the time that we can to stretch out these proceedings. The closer it gets to winter and the matter is still before the court, the less chance William has of being able to cross the Channel in an attack. Have Harkon see that a message is sent to Archbishop Wulfstan asking if he can come to the meeting of the Witan. Also, I want to be sure that the court applies English law to arrive at any decision it makes. He will know the law and how to be make certain this is the case."

March 18th, 1066
London, England

Harkon sat quietly observing as the leading men of England gathered for the meeting of the Witenagemot, the advisory council to the king. It was not the usual time for such a gathering, and it was only the fourth such gathering of which Harkon had been able to be a part. But William's court action had precipitated unusual needs that Harold thought best to discuss with the Witen. It wasn't a particularly large gathering—about twelve or so men—but it included some of the most powerful nobles and clergy of England as well as several wealthy, influential thegns. Most of them were aware in a general sense of the threat posed by William upon Harold becoming king. But only now that the Complaint had been filed would they learn the specifics of William's ambitions concerning England.

Harkon was fascinated by the workings, both grand and petty, of the Witen. As a hostage in Normandy, he had spent his younger years much as any youngster of good family would. But as he reached his teens, many of the rites of passage to adulthood were denied him. He was not given land to administer as he would have had he remained at home and a part of the most powerful family in England. He had not attended and ultimately become a part of the Witenagemot, the advisory council to the king. Instead, he watched as William exerted his autocratic rule over his comtes and vicomtes; observed how any advice which was not to William's liking was quickly abandoned before it could stir the ducal ire. The almost free-for-all atmosphere of the Witen, with men interrupting each other and expressing their opinions in loud voices, was still a process new to him.

Even now that he was home in England and had taken his rightful place as a member of the leading family in England and as nephew to the King, he remained more of an observer than a participant. And so he watched carefully as his king addressed the Witengemot with the news of William's court action. Should the other earls or prelates have particular questions regarding William, he was in a special position to attempt to answer them.

Harold gazed at the assembled nobles, prelates and thegns, raising his voice to be heard over the hub-bub. "Gentlemen, if I may have your attention. You have all received a copy of the Complaint filed by William, Duke of Normandy, in the AIC court. In essence, he seeks to have me deposed and become your King."

At this point Harold was interrupted by many voices loudly disclaiming any thought of William as king. Cries of, "No bastard can be king", "We have had enough of the Normans", "Who does William think he is?" reverberated throughout the chamber.

When order was restored, Harold continued, "William is contending that I swore an oath of fealty to him on holy relics and since, according to him, I have not kept my oath, I am foresworn and ineligible to become king. I must admit, I did swear an oath to him. However, it was an oath to be loyal to him as Duke of Normandy and to support his rightful claims in Normandy, as I had in the Brittany campaign. Further, the lives of my men, my younger brother and my nephew would be forfeit had I refused the oath. I told King Edward about it when I returned from Normandy and I also told Bishop Wulfstan. Both men agreed that I had no choice. However, if you did not already know of this oath, you need to be aware of it and the problems it presents to the safety of England. William is also alleging that King Edward promised him that he was his heir. We don't know whether Edward ever made such a promise, and if he did, when he might have said such a thing. Certainly we can no longer ask him about it," quipped Harold in an attempt to defuse the rising tension of the gathering.

"However, William's main contention is that such a promise is a *post obitum* gift and, as such, is irrevocable. While that may be the custom in Normandy, it is not the custom nor the law here. However, many of the judges of the court are from countries and principalities on the continent. Perhaps their homelands follow the Norman custom and interpretation. It will be critical to our defense that witnesses express our customs and laws regarding our procedures for a legitimate succession to the throne. Particularly important is the right of the monarch to revoke all such designation at any time and that any such prior designation is especially revoked if a different designation is made as a dying declaration, as was made by King Edward.

"In Count II of his Complaint, William has alleged that the deathbed designation of me as Edward's successor was obtained by 'undue influence'. Given the presence of Edward's doctors, his confessor, his wife and any number of other earls, I'm not sure how he could believe I somehow managed to 'force' King Edward to name me his successor, but nonetheless, that is what he has alleged.

"I bring this Complaint before you because I believe this is serious threat to England. We must do everything possible to defeat these claims in court. Those versed in law tell me that there is every likelihood that we will prevail."

As Harold laid out William's complaint so calmly and rationally, Harkon thought, *How like Harold. Ever the diplomat and negotiator. He doesn't even sound angry! If that were me, I think I'd sound a lot more upset than he does. But then, I suppose he knows these men well and I don't.*

"However, information has come to us that William has held a meeting with many of his allies and potential allies at Lillebonne with the aim of enlisting their aid in building, furbishing and manning a fleet suitable for an invasion of England," continued Harold.

As he said this, Harkon realized his assessment of Harold's demeanor had been a bit premature. There was now ample anger and determination in Harold's voice as he spoke of Lillebonne. As both Harold and Harkon knew, there was no reason to trust William's words. Devious was his middle name!

"Fortunately, the initial response was not very encouraging, but clearly William is serious about his claim to this throne, whether he gains it by court action or possibly invasion," concluded Harold.

At this point, Bishop Wulfstan of Worcester spoke up. "Your Grace, I believe I speak for the council when I say that every effort must be made to defeat William in this matter. There is no support for William as our king. It would violate every custom, tradition and law of England to accept his claim as having any foundation. Furthermore, if in spite of agreeing to abide by the decision of the Court, he builds a fleet to invade because he disagrees with the Court's opinion, then we shall strongly resist any such attempt to force his rule upon us." Bishop Wulfstan's words were met with resounding roars of approval by the gathered men.

"Before we adjourn, I want everyone to know that Earl Leofwine and Bishop Wulfstan will be working closely with me in the conduct of this suit brought by Duke William," Harold said.

As the witan members stood, stretched and broke up into groups of friends and went their separate ways, Harold beckoned to Bishop Wulfstan and Leofwine to join him. "Bishop, I would speak with you and Leofwine in private about William's Complaint. If you would join me now." He gestured for me to also follow as he strode down the halls and up the stairway to his private quarters. Leofwine, the Bishop and I all hurried to keep pace with his long strides.

Arriving at his chambers, Harold turned to the Bishop. "As I just mentioned, I would appreciate it if you would share your legal knowledge with Leofwine in drafting the answer to William's allegations. I am particularly concerned that the Court might make their decision based on the laws of the Flanders or Normandy rather than our laws. Can we do anything about that?"

Pausing a moment to catch his breath after nearly a sprint through the halls, and to gather his thoughts, Bishop Wulfstan replied, "Sire, my immediate thoughts would be to petition the court for a ruling as to the applicable law to be applied to each disputed issue, before any evidence is taken. In other words, right at the beginning of the proceedings. Leofwine and I would have to research the specific rules and procedures of the AIC court to determine precisely the correct form such a request would take, of course, but I am reasonably certain that such a procedure would be available to the parties."

"I agree with the Bishop, Harold," added Leofwine. "The rules and procedures I have reviewed so far, appear to allow requests to be made to the court in the form of motions. Given the importance of which country's laws should be used in determining the admissibility any evidence or determining the relevancy of testimony, I am certain that we could, and should, file a motion requesting a determination of which country's laws apply to decisions regarding each of the major issues. We could file such a motion at the same time that we answer the Complaint and request an immediate hearing before the Court to argue the motion.

"I don't think William has given thought to the importance of which country's law is to be applied, or he would have already addressed it by a motion. My guess would be that he assumes that because the court is in Flanders and Baldwin is his father-in-law, and the laws there are much the same as in Normandy, the laws and customs which he knows and is used to applying, will be the laws used to decide this dispute. Hopefully, the Court will see it as a conflicts of laws issue and apply the customary rules regarding such situations."

"Harkon, you need to be in on this, too," suggested Harold. "After all, you have spent nearly twelve years in Normandy, some of it present at William's ceremonies and courts. You can contribute some information regarding the substance of the usual Norman customs or laws that would be applied in various circumstances."

"Bishop Wulfstan, Harkon, would tomorrow afternoon be convenient for us to meet to go over the Complaint in detail and see about drafting this conflicts motion?" asked Leofwine.

"That would be fine, say right after the noon meal?" replied the Bishop, and Harkon added his assent.

"Good," responded Leofwine.

With that, the men left King Harold's chambers to begin their tasks. Harold, reassured by the tenor of the Witan and its receipt of the news of the Complaint, tried to relax as he reviewed the day's events. Stirring the fire to life, he thought it encouraging that the Witan clearly didn't want William as king, but then again, they were English. None of the judges of the Court hearing the matter, however, were English. Nor was it their country that might gain a bastard king!

Harold rose from the seat he had only just sat in, poured himself some wine, and while continuing to try to convince himself that all was as well as it could be, knew that the main issue, his oath, still loomed large. The problem of saving both England and perhaps his soul had yet to be resolved. His thoughts yet again circled round and round like an out of control merry-go-round, going nowhere. *Was William morally right when he alleged I was ineligible to accept Edward's nomination because I had sworn to support William in his endeavors? Would Bishop Wulfstan be able to find a legal and moral way out of this dilemma? How could he be so right and yet wrong at the same time?*

The days following the meeting of the Witan were difficult ones for Harold. As he went about the business of being king, his thoughts were never far from the conflicts engendered by his oath to William. The one non-negotiable fact was that the problems created by his oath of fealty could no longer be ignored or put aside. There were legal allegations published to his peers that had to be answered. His throne, and maybe his life, depended upon it. Again and again he argued with himself, asking, "How could I have done anything differently?" His inner self answered, *you could have stayed at home.* "True, but how was I to know we would be blown off course? It wasn't something that we planned to do. And I certainly wasn't anticipating being held by Guy of Ponthieu nor being 'rescued' by William!" he answered.

He so clearly remembered that last day in Normandy—a day he now thought of as a day of infamy. It had started out as a day to be remembered—they were going home. It had been bright, sunny, cool with only a slight breeze off the ocean, a perfect day for the feast William had planned. The successful campaign in Brittany was to be celebrated and William had finally arranged for a ship to take us to England. William had gifted me a suit of armor, in part as a token of his thanks for saving the lives of two of his men during the campaign and in part so I would be suitably attired when he knighted me. He had previously told me he wanted to do this, make me a knight of Normandy. Thinking about it now, my inner self asked the question I should have asked at that time: Why would William arrange to do this, or even want to knight me? We were equals, a Duke and an Earl, both vassals of our separate kings. But looking back, at that time, it had seemed a harmless show of friendship. How could I have been so naïve! I had been with William for several months. I had had ample opportunity to learn how devious and subtle he could be when planning to gain an objective.

Should I have been prepared for William's demand that I pledge an oath of fealty to him? Certainly it had never been mentioned as a required part of the knighting ceremony. Nor had anything been mentioned of the fact that it was to be sworn on not one but two sacred objects, a Holy Bible and a casket of holy relics. Did the sanctity of the oath override all other aspects of the situation, such as it having been 'commanded' by William, or that the safety of my brother and nephew, and that of my men were at risk if I refused to take the oath? The fact I had no knowledge that the covered casket contained Holy relics? William was now proclaiming to the world that the sanctity of the oath, the swearing of allegiance on holy relics was the only thing that mattered. None of the other circumstances counted in comparison with an oath taken before God. Was he right? Would the judges of the AIC agree with William's interpretation?

As Harold wrestled with the dilemma he and his country were in, the one thing he knew for certain was that the coming months would be challenging ones for all.

April 20th, 1066
Rome, Italy

Archdeacon Gilbert and his party, tired and enveloped in travel grime, arrived in Rome thankful to have made the journey without incident. Gilbert was glad they arrived late on a Saturday. That gave him a day to recover from the journey before he had to start on the Duke's business. A day of Mass and spiritual devotions would be welcome indeed.

After Mass Monday morning, Gilbert sought out Cardinal Giovanni, executive secretary to Pope Alexander II, to present his letters of introduction from Duke William and those from Abbot Lanfranc, a close friend of Pope Benedict II. He was received cordially. Arrangements were made for a meeting with Pope Alexander in two days, which would give the Pope and the Cardinal a chance to review Gilbert's documents.

When they all met two days later, Archdeacon Gilbert presented the request of William that the Pope support him in his claim as the rightful heir to King Edward of England. Armed with the arguments prepared by Abbot Lanfranc, he presented William's position as eloquently as he was able.

Over the course of the following week, Gilbert met with the Pope and sometimes separately with Cardinal Giovanni, Secretary to the Pontiff, to further discuss the situation, what actions William was presently taking and what further ones, if any, he might anticipate taking. The Cardinal-Secretary was full of questions regarding William's claims and in particular, exactly what actions did William expect of the Pope to show papal support?

After several days of meetings with Gilbert, the Cardinal-Secretary, the Pope and several other cardinals met in the Papal quarters to the discuss the implications of William's request for the Church, both politically and spiritually and to decide on a course of action, if any.

Pope Alexander II opened the meeting by saying to his advisors and friends what everyone was thinking but hadn't as yet put into words. "It's a heady thought that the Pope might create a king. Certainly such a thing would have enormous political implications. Would it set a precedent for the future? Would kings become kings only by the approval of the Pope? The battles for a determination of the supremacy of King or Pontiff has been going on for several years and is by no means resolved. Might support of William tip the balance in the Church's favor?"

"I admit, it's a tempting thought," agreed one of the Cardinals, "but how do we get around the argument that an archbishop, exercising the spirituality of his office, anointed and consecrated Harold as king? How do you undo that? If he hadn't been consecrated, it would be a different story. But aren't we supposed to be leading a reform of the Church and its practices, not adding to the abuses? We have always maintained that once consecrated, the ruler is in God's hands, not ours. From everything we have heard, Harold became king in accordance with the laws and customs of England. Can we overturn a country's legal procedures?"

Cardinal Giovanni spoke up. "On a very practical note, we need the monies that England tithes us each year. Openly support William and we can be sure that it will be the last we see of any yearly income from England. William suggests, Your Holiness, that you excommunicate Harold, I suppose because he is foresworn of his oath of fealty. I would suggest that If breaking an oath of fealty is grounds for being excommunicated, half of the members of the AIC would be excommunicated."

"Is there anything that he asks that we could give him?" asked the Pope.

"Well," volunteered Cardinal Giovanni, "William has put his case before the High Court of the AIC. We could file as a friend of the court. Essentially we would be arguing, or advising, the court of the Church's position on the nature of and rules about *post obitum* gifts and their irrevocability. If the court were to rule that the criteria for *post obitum* gifts, as we explained it to them, had been fulfilled, then William would be in the right, at least on that issue and the Church would have shown its support of him. "

"In the letter to me," said Pope Alexander, "William implies he will acknowledge the superiority of rights of the Papacy in church appointments. That would be a powerful tool for the Church. The problem is, can William be trusted in this? He didn't appear to have much trouble defying a Papal order that his marriage to Matilda was forbidden. He went ahead and married her anyway. If and when he is King of England, is he likely to remember how he got there and who made it possible? I'm very suspicious that he would not. He argues that he will spearhead the reforms needed in the Church in England. He mentioned Bishop Stigand as a prime example. But he has done nothing in his own backyard. His half-brother Bishop Odo is certainly not going to win any churchman of the year award. He is as disgraceful as Stigand.

""We'll meet again tomorrow morning to formalize the massage to be sent to Duke William. Archdeacon Gilbert wants to leave for home the following morning, We will plan to meet with him for the final time tomorrow afternoon and give him our answer at that time. In the meantime, pray for guidance on these issues."

April 22d, 1066
London, England

Wulfstan of Worcester arrived at the King's residence, weary but adamant that he must see King Harold immediately. Within several minutes he was escorted into the King's private quarters.

"Bishop Wulfstan, it's good to see you again. What brings you so urgently to London?"

"Sire, one of my priests who just arrived from Rome, had some news which I thought you should know about as soon as possible. On this priest's journey back to England, he and his group spent the night at a monastery which is a usual overnight stopping place for those going to and from Rome. At the same time, there was a party from Normandy on their way to Rome. Between the servant's conversations with each other, and my priest's inquiries, he was able to learn the purpose of the Normandy group's visit to Rome. At the command of Duke William, Archdeacon Gilbert of Lisieux was to try to persuade the Pope to support William's position that he was the rightful king of England."

"Before we discuss this any further, let me see if Leofwine and Harkon are close by to join us. While we are waiting, I'll have some food and drink prepared and you will have a chance to catch your breath from the journey here. Archdeacon Gilbert will only just about now have reached Rome. Unfortunately, there isn't time to get a message to our people in Rome to see what can be discovered about this mission—whether it is successful or not," commented Harold.

After Leofwine and Harkon joined them and been brought up to date with Bishop Wulfstan's news, Harold asked, "What do you think are Gilbert's chances of getting the Pope's support, Father? Or more importantly, what do you think can be done about this mission?"

Having had a chance to refresh himself, Bishop Wulstan answered thoughtfully, "It's important to note that to date, there appears to be no attempt to have your prelates or government participate in any way in the Pope's decision. Granted, it is early yet, but frankly, I doubt if any effort to involve England in any decision will happen. I also think that the Pope will have a problem with how he is to show his support of William, if that is what he decides to do. Advocating the removal of a king who was anointed by one of his own archbishops who has receive his pallium from Rome and is one of the mainstays of the English church would present a volatile political situation with the members of the High Court. Certainly they would think, if not outright ask, 'If it can happen to an anointed king, what about me?' It might also jeopardize Alexander's position. Remember, he has just survived several years of war and anti-pope struggles to solidify his own position. Such a controversial move to support William to remove or replace a king might well result in another rebellion to remove him."

"What are the chances that Pope Alexander might excommunicate Harold because of his supposedly broken oath to support William?" asked Leofwine, expressing the concern he felt for his brother and his King. "Excommunication is surely an action which is within the purview of the Church."

Bishop Wulstan thought about that course of possible action for a bit before he replied, "I believe the Pope has a problem in that regard also. If the promise to be his heir was made to William, it was made by King Edward. And he is the one who changed his mind and nominated Harold, not Harold. If anyone is foresworn, it would be King Edward."

"But isn't my uncle also foresworn for not supporting William's goals?" interjected Harkon.

"No, I don't think so," replied the Bishop. "Remember there are layers of obligations. The obligation to carry out the wishes of your King outweighs any obligation to a foreign duke, particularly when not within the realm of said foreign duke."

"So do you think he will do nothing, then?" asked Harold, beginning to hope this mission to the Pope just might amount to nothing and go away. Wulstan's answer dashed that hope quickly.

"I doubt he will do nothing. The Italian Normans have been very supportive of his papacy. I would bet he sympathizes with William's cause. My guess is that he will tell William privately of his support and publicly try to remain neutral. He also could show Church support by allowing a cleric/witness to testify as to the Church's position of *post obitum* gifts."

While this discussion went back and forth, Harkon was thinking, *And this is the Pope, the leading Christian in our world, that we are discussing! Since when are politics supposed to have any bearing on the state of your soul?* While he recognized the potential threat William's move represented to his uncle, he was thoroughly disgusted with the attempt, which just might be successful, at political maneuverings of the Papacy.

Harold spoke up. "It is too late to have any influence on the Pope's decision but I think that we must at least know what went on in Rome. Bishop, would you send a trusted messenger? Tell him to get there as quickly as he is able. Once there, have you someone in Rome in a position to find out what went on with the Norman delegation and what if anything was decided? Have your messenger meet with this person in Rome and return with any information he has been able to glean. As I said, it's too late to change anything, but with luck, a courier should be able to make the round trip well before the trial starts. There may be something we can use to our advantage at trial. At the very least, we would know if William's version of the trip is a truthful one."

April 27th, 1066
Rome, Italy

The final meeting of the Pope, his Cardinal-Secretary, Archdeacon Gilbert and his chief assistant clerk was held in the Pope's private conference chamber. While the Pope looked on in Papal serenity and superiority, Cardinal Giovanni presented the Church's position to Archdeacon Gilbert.

As Giovanni was explaining at great length the regard in which William was held, Gilbert's hopes of a successful conclusion to his mission dwindled and died. The bottom line was that the best the Pope could do would be give William a ring containing the hairs of a saint as a gift to show his regard and support. While the Pope personally agreed with William's claims, the matter was now before the High Court and the Church could not interfere in the legal procedures of a civil matter. If William decided to have a churchman testify as to the rule and meanings of a *post obitum* gift, of course, any bishop would be able to do that and would be happy to do so.

"The Church was in a difficult position," explained the Cardinal. Both England and Normandy were its children. As with any loving parent, one child could not be preferred over the other. As the loving earthly father of each, the Pope must maintain his public impartiality.

With no choice but to accept the papal decision, Archdeacon Gilbert and his party left Rome the following morning. Gilbert was looking forward to returning to Normandy but dreaded what he must report to Duke William. At least he had a month or so before he had to face what would most likely be a very angry and disappointed duke.

May 22d, 1066
London, England

Leofwine knocked at Harold's door, documents in hand. Upon being bid to enter, he said, "Harold, several new developments. First, as you know, William filed his reply to our motion early and did not request a hearing. We have just now received a notice that the court will not require oral argument. We have leave to request oral argument if we want to, so that's decision number one. Secondly, there is news of another meeting of William with his allies."

Harold pushed aside the documents he was reviewing, stretched, and rang for his steward. "Before we talk about this, let me get us something to eat to hold us until dinner. It's been a long morning and I'm starving."

After the steward brought food and drink, Harold continued, "About the oral argument: admittedly, his defense to the motion was pretty weak, but I think it more likely there was no hearing request because William figured out the strategy of delay. He knows that if he is going to invade England, he must launch his attack before the winter gales virtually close the Channel. If he doesn't have a really good argument for his position, why waste the time with an additional hearing? The question remains, do we want to orally argue? What are your thoughts on it?"

"Much as we would like a hearing to further delay the trial, there really isn't anything I could add in oral argument that hasn't already been said in the motion. Once courts have told you what they don't want or need, they tend to be unreceptive and put out if you contradict them by requesting what they don't want. So, looking at the pros and cons, plus the likelihood that they will grant the Motion, I would say we give up the delay option and do not request a hearing."

"Alright, we will await the court's decision on the motion. Now, what's this about another meeting of William's allies?"

"The latest word from our people in Normandy is that William has held yet another meeting to prepare for an invasion. These meetings are getting more successful in terms of gaining men and pledges but he doesn't have enough as yet. It's also getting increasingly difficult to keep these meetings, and particularly the purpose of them, from becoming known. William is well aware of the argument that could be made before the court that he is just going through the motions of a trial and has no intention of abiding by a court decision if he doesn't like it."

"Well, we always have that argument available, if we need it," agreed Harold. "In the meantime, there is not much that we can do about these meetings except keep track of them and note whatever progress William is making. Now, If that takes care of all the business, come, join me and Ealdgyth for dinner."

May 30th, 1066
London, England

Startled, Harold looked to the door as he realized some-one had been knocking. "Come," he called.

Leofwine entered in a rush, already speaking. "We have a problem, Harold, a serious one."

"Well, what is it?"

"In a word, Tostig!"

Shaking his head, Harold asked, "What has he done now? And why couldn't our father have lived long enough to pound some sense into his spoiled, willful head?" he muttered, half to himself.

"He's raiding along the southern coast—that's what he's done and is still at it. We don't have enough information yet to know if he has joined with William or Harald Hardrada or if it's his own idea, but the fact remains that there are villages and countryside in ruins as a result of his raids."

"How far as he gotten?"

"He seems to be working his way northward along the southern and eastern shores. Not too many raids have been carried out. Fortunately, the watches set to keep on the lookout for any action by William were able to get word to us quickly. But troops have to be sent to stop him before more damage is done. The problem is that he is landing, raiding for stores and valuables and going off to sea again before there is time to stop him."

"I don't have enough to worry about between William's suit, and Harald Hardrada making claims that England should belong to him, Leofwine, without our own brother turning traitor! Get hold of the local landowners along the coastline. Have them set up additional lookout posts to see if we can't spot in advance where it seems likely Tostig plans next to land. Tell them they are to be prepared to call out the local militia to repel any attempt by Tostig to land. Also, see what ships are nearby where he has been raiding. Send them orders to harass Tostig at sea, sinking any of his ships that they can."

As Leofwine left to do his bidding, Harold thoughts turned to the long, volatile summer that appeared to be ahead of him. Yet again his thoughts returned to the oath he had given to William. Could all these troubles be God's way of telling him he was foresworn? Even though Bishop Wulfstan had assured him of the legality of his actions, was it possible that being in the legal right wasn't enough? That it was the moral obligations which counted and he had failed in that duty? It was a sobering thought.

June 17th, 1066
Bayeux, Normandy

William and his brother, Bishop Odo, met to discuss the progress made in recruitment of men and monies at the recent meeting in Bonneville-sur-Touques.

"Odo." William raised his voice in frustration as he paced the room. "Something has to be done about the delays in getting the ships built! At this rate, we won't have enough until next season! We can't let Harold sit on my throne that long. It's bad enough that we have to hang around and wait while the Court ponders and debates, doing whatever courts do before they finally get around to making a decision on anything. But we must be ready to move as soon as the trial is over and a verdict announced—if that verdict is against us."

"I agree with you William, but everything is being done that can be. It takes time to build a fleet large enough to carry an invasion force of men and horses as well as supplies. There is a big difference between fighting in our own territory with land supply lines, and fighting on another's lands that are separated from our main support for supplies by a large body of water with fickle tides and winds."

They were interrupted by the arrival of a courier seeking William. Brought before William, he identified himself as from the AIC court and handed William several documents. William sent him off to the kitchens to refresh himself, He turned to Odo and said, "Well, read it. What have their lordships to say today?"

Odo, perused the documents. "They have granted England's Motion for Determination of Conflicts of laws. English law determines everything about the promise made by Edward to you as well as how a king is selected. But the oath of fealty issues are to be determined by Norman law, as we expected.

The other document is an Order setting the schedule for the exchange of exhibit information and the list of witnesses. The list of witnesses must be filed by July 14th and the exhibits must be exchanged by August 11th. The trial is scheduled to start the 20th of August. Well, at least there is finally a trial date. Even if the trial takes two weeks or so, and allowing another several weeks for the Court to reach a decision, there would still remain enough of the season to land in England, if that's what you decide to do."

"I had best get back to Rouen, then, let Richard know, and get him working on what will be needed for trial. Plan on joining Richard in ten days or so, say about the first of July. Both of you can go over what witnesses will be needed, as well as start to put together an exhibit list, whatever that is. I leave the details to you and Richard but the Court must understand that I am the rightful king of England. I will not be cheated out of what is rightfully mine and they had best recognize that!"

June 17th, 1066
Westminster, England

Leofwine entered Harold's study, proclaiming, "It's here. The Court has finally established a schedule and set a trial date. It has also granted our motion of jurisdiction. Now the serious work begins. First off, we need to determine who our witnesses are going to be. And, secondly, what documents do we need to place into evidence which will support the witnesses' testimony.

"There were three counts to William's Complaint," said Harold. "It is hard to know with which one he will start the opening testimony. For our planning purposes, let's assume he will first try to establish the promise by Edward. We have some advantage here since it is our law that applies. As I see it, William has a problem here. If the promise was made as part of a settlement to allow my father and the rest of us to return to England, it has to have been made in 1052. Edward, if he was naming William as his heir, would have wanted to ensure his choice by getting the consent of the Witan. The only person still alive who would likely have been part of the Witan at that time would be Archbishop Stigand. If there were others, no one seems to know who they were. Whoever they were, it is unlikely that they would come forward now since it would amount to supporting William as king. So, who except William or Stigand could or would testify that such a promise was made? Even if Stigand was called to testify all he could say is that the designation was made and he said he would support it when the time came to approve of a successor to Edward, assuming, of course that he was still alive. Even so, his would be only one vote of the members of the Witan that would be held at Edward's death, and he clearly would be outvoted. Besides, Leofwine, didn't our contact in Rome say something about William's envoy arguing that the Church in England needed to be reformed, using Stigand as an example of its excesses? I would think it very unlikely that Vos would chance having him come to Ghent to testify on William's behalf. It seems it will come down to William's testimony that such a promise was made, and William himself admits he wasn't even here in England when it was supposedly made."

"I agree with what you are saying, but I think we also have to establish to the court's satisfaction at this point that even if Edward made such a designation, it is superseded under English law by his deathbed declaration. And further, the fact it was not an irrevocable *post obitum* gift as William wants everyone to believe," said Leofwine. I would suggest either Bishop Wulfstan or Archbishop Ealdred of York testify to these issues. Archbishop Ealdred's testimony would probably carry the greater weight."

"I would like to meet with both of them as soon as possible, Leofwine. I know that Bishop Wulfstan said we had a legal defense to the oath of fealty argument, but I am still very worried about how the Court will react to that issue. See when either or both of them can get to London and plan on you and I conferencing with them about these issues."

After the meeting with Leofwine, and while awaiting the arrival of Bishop Wulfstan and Archbishop Ealdred, Harold continued to worry the issue of his oath like a faithful terrier ridding his master's territory of a captured rodent. While going about the business of being king, he had to keep telling himself that Bishop Wulfstan would not have allowed the Answer to be submitted without good legal cause. But his own regard of the oath continued to eat away at his self-esteem and soul.

Finally, Bishop Wulfstan and Archbishop Ealdred arrived in London to discuss further the defense of these issues at trial. Harold was both optimistic and fearful of the outcome of their meeting: optimistic that the plan of defense of the oath of fealty would be settled, in his favor, but fearful that despite the legal affirmative defense made, the churchmen would be unable to establish sufficient moral grounds to absolve his actions.

Harkon, as Harold personal attendant, was present when Archbishop Ealdred and Bishop Wulfstan met with Harold in his chambers at the castle. Having been at Bonneville-sur-Tourque on that fateful day when Harold swore the oath of fealty to William, Harkon was particularly interested in what the prelates had to say about it.

"Archbishop Ealdred, Bishop Wuflstan, thank you for making your journey here. I know it was a long one, especially for you Archbishop. York is a long way from London," said Harold . "Leofwine and I have been discussing the strategy of the defense to be presented at trial. It appears to us there are two major issues that would be dealt with best by your testimonies. The first is the definition of and procedures involved, as a practical matter and as a matter of law, of *post obitum* gifts in England. Any testimony will also focus on the irrevocability of such a gift, as well as the priority, if any, of a deathbed nomination of heir. The second issue is how the matter of my oath of fealty to William is defended. I know we discussed it somewhat, Bishop Wulfstan, at the time of drafting our answer to the Complaint, but the time has now come to deal with it in a more complete manner."

Archbishop Ealdred offered, "I am certain the testimony that can be offered regarding a *post obitum* gift under our customs and laws will not be to Duke William's liking. I'm aware from my contacts with other prelates that in Normandy ducal succession and post obitum gifts are often closely related, but here in England where land ownership is held very

74

differently from that of France, the connection doesn't apply. Here, not all title to land originates with the king. As a result, King Edward couldn't 'gift' 'all the lands of England' over which he was king because he didn't have title to all the lands of England. Unlike Normandy, wherein all the lands now known as Normandy were granted to Rollo by the French king, English lands result from an amalgamation of kingdoms and leaders, and conquest by Viking raiders, ultimately resulting in the acknowledgment of one king as ruler, but not necessarily as the single supreme landholder. This supreme king could nominate an heir, but such a nomination certainly was revocable, subject to changes which might occur with the passage of time and circumstances. Most importantly, his choice might not be accepted by the Witen! Leofwine and I can go over the particularities to establish the revocability and formulation of naming an heir and develop the specific testimony required at Leofwine's convenience. Also, there are formalities of gifting that must be present, which are totally absent in William's case."

Bishop Wullfstan, reaching for a document among his papers and handing it to Harold, said, "Sire, in conjunction with our earlier conversations regarding a defense to your oath, I have brought a copy of a letter from Bishop Fulbert written in 1020. It is accepted by legal scholars as the definitive word on the subject. I believe it answers all your questions and any questions the Court may have on the issue."

Harold took the letter and read it carefully. He nearly leaped to his feet as the meaning of Fulbert's words became clear to him. Trying to maintain a regal demeanor even though he felt like turning cartwheels, he said, "This letter can prove that I'm not foresworn! Until this moment, even after all the trial preparation discussions...even after going over all the issue and facts and possible testimony, I never dared hope there was an answer to having given that oath of fealty. Now I see that the answer is right there in front of me." Handing the letter to Leofwine for his review, Harold inquired, "Will there be any difficulty in presenting this letter to the Court?"

Bishop Wulfstan turned to include Leofwine in his reply. "While what I have is merely a copy, the Bishop of Chartres has a copy in his records that I believe would be accepted by the Court into evidence. No one can produce the original since it was delivered to William V, Duke of Aquitaine. I would expect that William's counsel will try to keep it from being admitted into evidence but I don't believe he will prevail. What do you think, Leofwine?"

"I agree" replied Leofwine. "We can call the bishop to testify, which shouldn't be a problem since he is still in Chartres and can be subpoenaed to court. Since he is in charge of the official records of Chartres, he can authenticate it as a true copy of the Church official records."

At this point, Harold spoke up saying, "Gentlemen, I leave you to your further discussions of these trial intricacies as I must attend to other matters which have arisen. Leofwine, I will hear your report when I return in several days. Archbishop Ealdred and Bishop Wulfstan, I truly appreciate your help in resolving these issues."

Several hours later, Harold and his troop left London headed for Bosham. He had to restrain himself from galloping the entire way. He couldn't get to Edith Swanneck fast enough to share the good news. Aside from Harkon, Leofwine and Bishop Wulfstan, only Edith had been aware of the turmoil and doubts within him since he accepted the throne. He had shared with her his dilemma, now he couldn't wait to share with her the resolution and his relief.. While his relationship with his new Queen was cordial and he accorded her all the courtesies and ceremony due to her, she did not hold the keys to his heart; she was not his soul mate. Edith was his one love.

July 3d, 1066
Rouen, Normandy

Bishop Odo and Richard Vos were gathered in William's office chamber at the castle awaiting the arrival of William.

William entered the room, cordially greeting everyone. "We finally have a court date and now we can get something done. I have asked you to attend me in order to plan the strategy of this trial. We need to discuss who will be the witnesses, what they will say in court, and what documents will be needed to support their testimony. Speaking of witnesses, Richard, have we heard from Archdeacon Gilbert yet?"

"He has just returned from Rome. I asked him to join us this afternoon to report on his meetings," replied Richard.

William continued, "As I see it, there are three main issues which the Court must decide in our favor: Edward' gift to me was an irrevocable promise, Harold's oath to me was a fraud, and, by trickery and undue influence Harold made himself king me. If this essentially sums up our position, Richard, how do you intend to convince the Court in the strongest way possible that the coronation of Harold is void and of no legal account?"

"Let's start with the promise made by Edward," Vos said. "I would expect that we should consider calling a churchman as an expert, regarding a *post obitum* gift. Then we have to decide what witnesses we could call to support your position We need to present evidence as to the circumstances surrounding that gift. For instance, did King Edward tell you that you would be his heir when you were in England in '51?"

"No, not at that time. That was just a short trip to discuss not giving harbor to the Norsemen who were again raiding the English coastline. Edward hinted that he was considering naming me as his heir but didn't say anything definite at that time. In '52, when Archbishop Robert returned to Normandy, he told me that the return of the Godwines from exile had been negotiated. Edward named me his heir, and as part of the settlement, the earls who were present and comprised a Witan, agreed to support his choice of me. Godwine also gave his son and grandson as hostages, who were brought to me by Archbishop Robert when he returned to Normandy. That's when he told me that Edward had declared me his heir. He said it was partly because of all the years my father and I sheltered Edward and his brother while in exile—"

"Who were these members of the Witan, did he say?"

"Yes, he said there was Godwine himself, the Earls of Northumbria and Mercia, Bishop Stigand, and some other wealthy thegns whose names he didn't know. The hostages were given to assure that Godwine would honor Edward's designation of me."

"Are these northern earls still alive?" asked Bishop Odo.

"According to my sources in England," William answered, "both of the northern earls have died and have now been succeeded by their sons."

"Well, that presents a problem. Everyone then, except Stigand, is dead, and Stigand is in England. While we could require his attendance, I do not think he would be a very credible witness. William, it's unfortunate that Archbishop Robert is no longer with us. I don't know what else we can do to establish that Edward named you as heir other than to have you testify to it."

"Of course I will testify to this!" snapped William, rising so suddenly from his chair that it fell backwards. "And the Court will believe it! Who is there to prove he didn't name me his heir?"

Even as he said this, William was thinking, even if they didn't believe him, his fleet was nearing completion.

Simmering down slightly, he added, "Well, be sure you also call Brother John. As my secretary, he was present when Archbishop Robert stopped at the castle on his way to Rome and delivered the hostages and told me.

"I agree," said Vos. "That could be very helpful. Father John would be a credible witness."

Changing the subject, hoping William would remain in an affable mood, Richard asked, "Who would you suggest as an expert, Bishop Odo, to establish the naming of the heir as a *post obitum* gift?"

"Abbot Lanfranc would be the obvious choice but I wonder if he can be depended upon to stick to just that one issue. He is such a scholar that we might get an academic dissertation on all the kinds of gifts to the Church, additional testimony we'd just as soon not have," replied Odo. "Still and all, he is the obvious choice, and has the most prestige. How about Archdeacon Gilbert?"

Richard spoke up. "I only spoke with him briefly, but I had the sense that all did not go well in Rome. If that is the case, then we don't want him anywhere near the court. We'll know more this afternoon. In the meantime, we can think about it and perhaps Gilbert will have some ideas."

William stridently interrupted, "Richard, did you find out what the English rule or law is about *post obitum* gifts? Since their law applies, we need to know how they plan to defend the issue.

"Also, find out which of our comtes or vicomtes were present when Harold took his oath at Bonneville-sur-

Touques. While nobody was close enough to hear everything that was said, they all saw that an oath of fealty was given and can testify to that much. They can also testify as to the words of a Norman oath of fealty since they each have sworn one to me. My brother Robert was there, pretty close to Harold and me; call him as a witnes."

"Richard," he continued, since it will be our laws which apply, someone has to explain the intrinsic obligations of a Norman oath of fealty. Who do you have in mind to use as an expert or this? I don't know what the English believe, or what Harold thought he was swearing to, but it doesn't really matter.

"Lanfranc might be just the one for this," said Richard. "It would be just the sort of scholarly debate or instruction he would love to expound on. And, it would be relatively easy to keep him focused on just this issue. His testimony shouldn't open up extraneous issues that Leofwine could exploit on cross-examination."

At this point, William adjourned the morning's meeting. "Come, it's time for dinner. Matilda's displeasure will far outweigh her diminutive size if we are late. Let's meet afterwards to hear what Archdeacon Gilbert has to say of his mission to Rome."

Later that afternoon, when William, Vos and Bishop Odo resumed their strategy session they were joined by Archdeacon Gilbert.

Vos, having already forewarned William that the news was not very good, was not looking forward to this meeting. If the news was as bad as he expected, dealing with William's temper would be challenging.

"Well, Gilbert," William barked as they all sat down at the table, "bottom line, will the Pope support me or not?"

Gilbert, startled by the Duke's tone, stammered, "Yes and no, Milord."

"What kind of an answer is that?" demanded William. "I asked you a simple question. Yes and no, is not an answer!"

"What I meant, Milord, is that Rome will not directly support your cause but neither will they condemn it. The Church will not approve of deposing Harold since he is an anointed king. The Pope also doesn't believe there are sufficient grounds for excommunication. However, Rome is anxious to clean up the English church, so if you were to do that, they would approve of it. Although the delegation had many meetings with several influential cardinals, we could not get enough backing to have positive action taken by the Pope. The best that we could do was to get agreement that the Church would essentially remain neutral in the matter. The Pope personally was supportive of you and he sent you a ring with a hair of St Peter in it to show his support."

"Well, that's something but a banner to be flown would have been a more visible indication of support. Certainly not what you were expected to achieve, but better than nothing," grumbled William.

Dismissing Gilbert, William turned to Vos. "Well, At least the Church is not condemning action on my part. So, where do we go from here?"

Richard responded, "Well certainly that is one witness we won't be calling! I must talk to the men we have mentioned about testifying, and obtain any documents or exhibits needed to support their testimony. In particular, I should speak with Abbot Lanfranc to review his testimony. The witness list is the first thing that has to be done since it must be exchanged with England and submitted to the Court. I am sure that, as preparations progress, other witnesses and issues will come to mind that will require inclusion in our presentation of the case. But for now, this has been a productive start."

After everyone had left the meeting, William sat pondering his options. *The more this court thing goes on, the more useless it appears. It takes forever to get the simplest thing accomplished and when the Court does decide, it has not been in my favor. Thank the stars I have ships being built and Odo and Robert continue to help gather men. I may well have need of both.*

Later that evening, after William's storyteller had restored some semblance of good humor to William at dinner, he and Matilda discussed the day's events.

"It's all so simple," said William. "Edward named me his heir, just as my father named me his heir. Now I am Duke of Normandy, and I should already be King of England! Naming an heir is not something you can take back. Once it's done, it is done. Why can't they see that? Vos acts as if there is some big problem because there is no one but me to testify that Edward said I was his heir. Well, so what? I do say he named me and there isn't anyone who can say differently. And that designation is irrevocable! It stands."

At this point, Matilda spoke up. "William, what you say is certainly the usual situation here in Normandy, but do you know for certain, that it is the same in England? Richard is only trying to protect you by bringing out all the possible objections that might be raised at the trial. I know you don't want to hear it, but he is only doing his job."

"Personally, I prefer the job Odo and Robert are doing, raising troops and getting ships built!" William responded. "The longer this goes on, the more I regret that I ever agreed to put this matter before the Court. All they do is waste time; time I need if I am to get across the Chanel without being shipwrecked."

"William, you know you can't just invade England. Granted, it worked in Maine, but a bordering vassal duchy of France is not the same as the independent kingdom of England."

"Matilda, you know I had to do what I did. It was politically necessary for the safety of Normandy. Even though Walter of the Vixen was the heir, Normandy needed to secure its southern borders. It wasn't my fault and it couldn't be helped that Walter and his wife died while in Norman custody. Edward would, or should have, understood that."

"May he should have, but I'd venture to say that it will be brought up at the trial that he didn't and was very angry about his nephew dying while in Norman custody."

Avoiding further comment on a sore subject, William continued, "Matilda, can you believe how ineptly Archdeacon Gilbert handled the mission to Rome? Even after Abbott Lanfranc spent all that time with him, hand-feeding him the arguments needed, he still was unable to get any public indication of the Pope's support. Think about this. If the Pope doesn't condemn my claim, and I say he supports it, do you think Rome will openly contradict me? Rome wants England reformed. If I win this case, they know I will work with them to get it done, especially regarding Bishop Stigand. Granted, we didn't get a banner to prove Rome's support, but do we really need one?"

"I think there is a risk here, William. What if Harold calls Archdeacon Gilbert as a witness, and questions him about the trip to Rome? That is, if they know about it. Do they?"

"I'm not sure. I will have to ask Richard if he knows if Harold learned of Gilbert's mission. Certainly, England didn't respond to anything, or participate in any meeting, while Gilbert was in Rome. Even if they do know about it, what if Odo or Lanfranc or someone arranges to have Gilbert out of the country at the time of trial? That should solve any problem of his testifying. I had better speak with Richard about Gilbert's mission and preventing his possible testimony first thing in the morning."

July 8th, 1066
Bosham, England

Harkon was still removing his things from his horse when Harold, weary though he was from the ride, was already entering the hall calling boisterously for Edith.

Having heard the troop arrive, she appeared. Rushing to her and swinging her in his arms, he exclaimed, "You won't believe what Ealdred has been able to accomplish! I'm not foresworn!"

Harkon thought what a lucky man Harold was to have someone like Edith at his side. It wasn't often a man and woman managed to have such a loving relationship. Although he had to admit, it appeared that his grandmother and grandfather Godwine had also been close friends as well as husband and wife. Not that the Church saw Edith as a wife, but she certainly was as far as Harold was concerned.

"Harold, first, put me down. Let me get you and Harkon something to eat and drink, and then tell me what this is all about."

Harold did as she asked, but couldn't contain his enthusiasm enough to actually sit down and eat. Instead, he strode about the hall, drink in hand, while he told Edith about his meeting with Archbishop Ealdred and Bishop Wulfstan.

"I feel like the weight of the world has been lifted from my shoulders. I am the rightful king and will prove it to everyone. William will be shown to be the lying, grasping, power-hungry person that he really is."

"Well, this is certainly wonderful for you, not that I ever doubted for a moment that you were anything but the rightful king. But really, what happens next? Where do you go from here?"

"The Court has set a schedule for exchange of witnesses, experts, documents and the like and it has also set the 21st of August as the trial date. We were hoping we could delay until later than that, but it was not to be. However, the trial will take a week or more and who knows how long the justices will take to render a decision. We might possibly stretch out the trial until the winter season is upon us, making any alternative action by William impossible until spring, I really don't trust him to just accept the Court's decision if it goes against him. If the decision were to go against us, I doubt our people would accept it. Even if I stepped down in accordance with the decision, I don't think they would accept William without a battle.

"In the meantime, it appears that the next two months will be busy ones. I doubt I will have many opportunities to come to Bosham, much as I would like to be here. Let's make the most of what time I have now to enjoy each other and the children."

July 8th, 1066
River Dives Harbor, Normandy

William drew rein on the road where it reached a point it overlooked the meander loop of the river Dives and the harbor created there. As he surveyed the estuary and harbor, he thought with pleasure and pride of the victorious campaign against the armies or France and Anjou in 1057, won at this site. Now, he saw a vast fleet gathered there to carry out his plans to add England to his domains. There were still more ships, not yet arrived, to be gathered and further plans to be perfected, but in the event the AIC court did not support him, he was ready.

His brothers, Bishop Odo and Comte Robert, greeted him when he arrived at the castle. "Welcome William. Come, food and drink are all laid out, and waiting for you. We'll go over the details of the fleet after you have refreshed yourself."

Holding in his mind the satisfying picture of his fleet gathered in the harbor, and sorely in need of food and drink after his long ride, William gratefully accepted the urgings of Odo.

The following morning the brothers met to review the progress made in the invasion plans and to discuss actions that remained to be taken.

"One issue that must be addressed and taken seriously is how this large assembly of divers forces is to be provisioned. These final preparations will still take time. I will not have the countryside devastated while the men are quartered here!

Generous provisions must be made for our own knights and those from other parts, as well as for the rank and file troops. Make it known that the penalties will be severe for anyone violating my orders on this."

William did not feel it necessary to explain to his brothers his reasons for such an order. He, however, knew that large-scale devastation of the countryside by knights and men gathered in preparation for an invasion with an armada of ships, would quickly carry to the ears of the judges of the Court. He most definitely did not want to be in the position of having to explain to the Justices the purpose of this fleet amassed at Dives. If the Court ruled in his favor, well and good, the fleet could always be put to another purpose. If not, then he would be ready to enforce his claim.

July 13th, 1066
London, England

Entering his brother's chamber, Leofwine looked closely at Harold and smiled. "You appear ten years younger, Harold. Edith did wonders for you."

"She usually does," replied Harold, "but truly, I think mostly it is as a result of Archbishop Ealdred's words, which is what I wanted to talk to you about. The letter he spoke of is in the records at Chartres and the custodian of them is there. Also, the archdeacon they sent to Rome is in Normandy. As soon as we produce a list of witnesses, what is to prevent William from seeing to it that they are unavailable or unable to come to Court? After all, they are in his territory."

"I think the answer to that is we will have to have these witnesses served subpoenas from the Court, which would command them to appear at the trial. We would serve subpoenas in any event, but usually not until just before the date of trial. Considering the point you just raised though, I think we have to get these subpoenas served immediately."

"Will that accomplish our aim?" queried Harold.

"Once the subpoena is served, it's a court order to appear at the time and place stated. If William tries to hide these men after they have been served, he will be interfering with a court order.

"The real question is should I be there when the subpoena to Archdeacon Gilbert is delivered and take his deposition to discover what his testimony will be or just have the it served? The problem with my being there is, of course, then William will be aware of it, and Vos naturally would be at the deposition. If I don't go, at trial we would have no advance knowledge of what he will say. Called as a witness, he would be under oath and be required to answer any questions. Clearly, he would try to put a spin on his testimony to William's advantage. Even so, I don't believe he will actually lie under oath in court."

"I don't think that we need to take his deposition," said Harold. "I have just heard from Bishop Wulstan about our courier to Rome. He told Wulstan that our people in Rome say the Pope would not publicly state his approval of William's arguments. He didn't excommunicate you; he didn't declare you a usurper; he didn't absolve the English people from their obedience to you as king, and he didn't lay any interdict on Bishop Stigand. Nor, by the way, did the Pope say he would no longer accept the bountiful Peter's Pence paid to Rome each year by England. He did send a ring with St. Peter's hair in it to show his unofficial support of William's claim's, however.

"I can see it's a risk to question a witness when you don't really know what he is going to answer," continued Harold thoughtfully, "but compared to William's knowing that we are going to call Gilbert as our witness, and his knowing by a deposition what Gilbert is going to say, I think it is a risk we have to take. Send a courier to serve the subpoena immediately. If Gilbert notifies William, there isn't much we can do about it. But, at least he will have been served and will be required to show up in court. Hopefully, as an archdeacon of the church, he will testify truthfully."

"Even though there is no real problem with Bishop Robert of Tours as a witness, it would still be best to also have him served early with a subpoena *duces tecum*," added Leofwine. "He is an acknowledged legal scholar in his own right as well as being Bishop of Chartres. As such, he is the custodian of the records at Chartres, and able to authenticate Bishop Fulbert's letter as a true record of the Church. Adding the *duces tecum* to the subpoena requires him to bring Fulbert's letter to court with him. William will have a difficult time disputing the authenticity of Fulbert's letter. There isn't much he can do but try to block its admission, but I would expect the Court to admit it as a relevant document and a true copy. I wouldn't want to give William the opportunity to prevent Robert from testifying either. I will send a courier to the Court for the subpoenas today. Then If crossing the Channel goes well, which it should this time of year, the Bishop and Archdeacon should be served no later than ten days or so from today—before we have to disclose our witness list to the Court, and to William."

"Our witnesses then, are going to be Archbishop Ealdred regarding the oath of fealty, Bishop Robert of Tours to authenticate Bishop Fulbert's letter. Archdeacon Gilbert of Lisieux to testify to the non-support of Rome, and then, who else?" asked Harold.

"I was thinking Earl Mocar might be a good witness to explain the succession customs and laws. He certainly understands the concept of a ruler ruling in accordance with the law since he revolted against Earl Tostig but not against King Edward. He also was there when Edward died and heard his dying declaration. He was in a position to know that you were not near enough to Edward to have forced him to make that choice. While he is your brother-in-law, he wasn't at the time Edward died, nor will he be shy about saying that he had no great love for Godwine or his sons. In addition, he was part of the Witan that approved you as Edward's successor and saw you anointed and crowned as King of England. I just remembered," Leofwine added. "Archbishop Ealdred will also have to testify that he was the one who anointed and consecrated you as king. While Bishop Stigand was assisting, he was not the primary churchman. I don't think that Stigand would add anything to the trial as a witness, given his disputes with Rome."

"What do you think about calling our sister, Queen Edith as a witness, Harold? My thoughts are that she could establish that after our father and the rest of us returned in '52, she resumed the marital relationship with Edward, and potentially could have become pregnant. She also was involved in urging that the Aetheling be found and brought from Hungary. She certainly was intimately involved with the raising of young Edgar after his father died. Her testimony would be very strong evidence that even if Edward told William he was his heir in '52, which I don't believe he did, Edward did not consider such a designation as irrevocable. If he had not believed he could change his mind later, he would never have sent Archbishop Ealdred to Poland to negotiate entering Hungary to persuade Edward the Atheling to return to England. Nor would he have ordered you to escort him and his family to England on your return from Rome."

Harold replied, "I think she will testify. She really would rather have had the regency of young Edgar, but she recognizes that in today's political realities, a child king is not to be. And she surely does not want William in England. I think it a good idea."

"One other witness I think we should call," added Leofwine, "would be another churchman to testify that Rome had no pressing commitment to reform the English church. William is likely to try to paint the entire English church as riddled with prelates like Bishop Stigand and needing a thorough restructuring, which William would provide with the Pope's support. Unfortunately for William, his own half-brother, Bishop Odo exhibits every bit as much un-churchman-like habits and behavior as Bishop Stigand. I don't have anyone in mind right now, but I'll find someone we can call. Unless some surprise happens that we haven't planned on and we need to produce a rebuttal witness, the rest of the trial testimony will be cross-examination of William's witnesses in his case-in-chief and, of course, your testimony, Harold."

The following day, while Archbishop Ealdred was still in London, he and Leofwine met again to discuss his upcoming testimony at trial. They discussed Bishop Fulbert's letter, how it would be introduced by the Bishop of Chartres and authenticated and then what it meant, in general and particularly in regard to Harold's oath of fealty to William.

In the midst of these discussions, Archbishop Ealdred asked Leofwine, "Are you aware of the Papal Delegation's pronouncement in 786 regarding the eligibility of kingship in England?"

"What are you referring to?" asked Leofwine.

Archbishop Ealdred explained about the Papal Legate's decree when the Papal legates visited the court of Offa of Mercia in 786. "The decree stated that an English king 'must not be begotten in adultery or incest' and that 'he who was not born of a legitimate marriage' could not succeed to the throne. It is likely that there was no succession rule regarding bastards prior to this decree. But there certainly has been no bastards upon the throne since this decree," he explained.

Leofwine was jubilant. "How is it that I was not aware of this?"

Ealdred shrugged his shoulders. "I suppose because the issue has never come up since then."

"Oh, the justices will have fun with this one!" he exclaimed. "Your Grace, you are a font of information!"

With that, the meeting broke up, and Leofwine went to Harold to report what had transpired, and specifically to tell him the good news about the Papal Decree.

July 25th, 1066
Conches en Ouche, Normandy

The Vicomte de Conches was reviewing the current financial status of his holdings when his bailiff entered to announce the arrival of Archdeacon Gilbert of Lisieux with a request to speak with him. Although an unexpected visitor, Richard welcomed the excuse to cease reviewing dry manor reports and figures.

"Gilbert, a pleasure to see you. Come, sit down. Food and drink will be here momentarily. So, what brings you here so unexpectedly?" Richard asked.

Archdeacon Gilbert, clearly upset and distraught, handed Richard a paper. "A courier arrived at the cathedral the day before yesterday with this. It says I must appear at court as a witness for the English king! How can that be? Do I really have to appear as it states? What will Duke William say?" What if he thinks I asked to be Harold's witness?" The questions tumbled out almost faster than Gilbert could vocalize them. Certainly faster than Vos could answer.

"Gilbert, collect yourself," Richard ordered. "Give me a minute to read this and see what it is all about."

With difficulty, Gilbert remained silent, although it was beyond him to sit quietly. He paced about the chamber while Richard finished reading.

"Alright, Father, you are correct. This is a subpoena from the Court at the request of the defendant. It requires that you appear at court on the trial dates, as a witness to be examined by defendant's counsel. And yes, you must obey it. I just received a few days ago the list of the defendant's witnesses with your name on it, which I have sent on to Duke William, but I was unaware a subpoena had also been served."

"Couldn't I go somewhere so I wouldn't be available to be at Court?"

"That would have been possible if you had left before you were able to be served. However, not to appear would be a contempt of court for which the Court could, and likely would, impose a punishment. As to what the Duke will say, I believe that we are just about to find out. If I am not mistaken, that commotion in the bailey heralds the arrival of the duke and his men."

Vos had barely completed his sentence when Duke William stormed into the office, bellowing, "Vos, what is the meaning of this? Harold's list of witnesses says Gilbert of Lisieux will be a witness for him!" Upon sighting Gilbert, William came to an abrupt halt, and barked, "Gilbert, what are you doing here?"

Before the Archdeacon could say anything, which he was in no hurry to say in any event, Vos intervened. "William, he is here about the same matter that you are."

"Well, he won't be here for the trial! I have urgent business elsewhere that only he can attend to at that time, so he can't testify," challenged William.

"It's' too late for that now, William. He is on notice and under court order to appear on those dates."

Unhappily admitting defeat, at least for the moment, William sought his cup of wine and said, "What can we do about this, then?"

"Gilbert and I will have to carefully prepare for his testimony," answered Vos. "It is obvious the testimony Harold is looking for has to do with the mission to Rome this spring. But I don't think Gilbert's testimony will harm our argument.

It might have been more helpful if no one challenged what we say was the Pope's position, but the Pope never came out and publicly denied your claim to England's throne. It can certainly be argued that, at the very least, Rome is neutral about the matter."

Realizing that William still had an agenda of matters on his mind, Vos poured himself some wine and awaited William's next outburst. He didn't have to wait long.

"What's this nonsense about Bishop Robert of Tours being listed as a witness for Harold?" William asked in a voice that indicated the answer had better be a good one, or else.

"I must admit, listing Bishop Robert has me worried, if only because I can't imagine any reason Harold would want his testimony on anything," replied Vos. "I haven't hear anything from Robert yet, but my guess would be if they subpoenaed Gilbert, they have also subpoenaed the bishop's appearance. As soon as I hear from him, which I expect I will if he also has been served, I should have better information regarding what they hope to gain from his testimony. In the meantime, they have effectively guaranteed his appearance at trial."

Both William and Archdeacon Gilbert joined Vicomte Vos and his family for the main meal before resuming their return journeys. However, it was hardly a festive occasion. Although Vos played the part of host to his duke well, he was concerned with Harold's witness list. He also was chagrined that he had not acted more swiftly to get Gilbert beyond the reach of a subpoena.

William was in no mood to be a congenial guest. He had no qualms about being disinclined to engage in polite conversation with his vassals when he had other matters on his mind. Today, he was reliving the day's events, a review which did not please him. He was angry at Vos. After all, he reminded himself, it wasn't as if they hadn't envisioned the possibilities of the effect of Gilbert's testimony. They had. And as much as he was angry with Vos, he was furious Harold had bested him by this early service.

William was not accustomed to being bested in anything. It was especially galling that Harold had done so in securing the Gilbert's testimony. Testimony that would likely prevent William from having other leaders accept his version of Rome's support. As to Bishop Robert's testimony, who knew what Harold sought to gain from that? But whatever it was, he was William's vassal to order when and where to appear, not Harold's!

As for Archdeacon Gilbert, he contributed as little as possible to the high table's conversations. The less he was noticed by Duke William the happier he was. He was already worried about being a witness. No matter what Vicomte Vos said, he envisioned no good outcome from it. Whatever he said was bound to upset someone, probably William, a most dangerous person to cross. He eagerly anticipated the morning when he could escape for now, at least, to the sanctuary of his cathedral.

August 6th, 1066
London, England

Leofwine arranged to meet Harold to review the exhibits that England intended to submit to the Court at trial. "It's not a very long list, Harold. But I expect Vos will be prepared to argue about the admittance of most of the exhibits. The one I am most sure he would like to keep out of evidence is the Papal Legate's decision about bastardy, and I think that is the one on which he has the least likelihood of prevailing. It's possible, but not really likely, he will succeed in keeping the archive copy of Bishop Fulbert's letter out of evidence. Even if he did, there remains testimony from credible witnesses regarding the parameters of an oath of fealty, so the lack of the exhibit wouldn't be particularly harmful. Other than these two documents, I don't believe that there is anything else that needs to be introduced to support our defense. Anything you think of?"

"You're the one with the expertise for legal procedure, so if you say this is all we need, that's fine with me. What happens next?"

"We forward our list, such as it is, to the Court and to William, and he does the same with any list of exhibits he wants to introduce. When he receives our exhibits, he will advise the Court if he objects to their entry into evidence. I suspect it will probably be both of them. William will, in turn, do likewise. If we object to any, we tell the Court which one(s). If we don't object, then the Court will allow it to be marked as an exhibit prior to trial and later, at the appropriate time at trial, it will be accepted into evidence. Any exhibit that is disputed, will be argued by Vos and me at trial at as to its admissibility.

We should hear from Richard Vos soon with his objections on William's behalf. I doubt if he has any exhibits to be introduced. Since William doesn't read or write, he doesn't rely very much on documents. He is more of an "action" type.

"In any event, I will send the courier off with our list to William and the Court immediately to be sure the list is filed on time."

August 11th,1066
Rouen, Normandy

The servant found William at the stables admiring his newest foal. He delivered the message that the Viconte de Conches had arrived and was waiting to see the duke in the duke's office. William completed giving his instruction for the care of the new foal and then hastened inside to greet Vos.

"Richard, whatever brings you here, before you leave you must see the new colt. He is a beauty. If he grows up to be half the horse as his sire, he will be magnificent! But I suppose you have more serious matters to put before me than admiring a beautiful, healthy colt! So what is it now?"

"We have received the list of documents that the English want to place into evidence at trial. While I will object to all of them one in particular is disturbing."

"Read it to me and tell me why it is important."

Godwineson is alleging that it is a document from Papal Legates visiting at the court of Offa of Mercia in 786 which declared that 'he who was not born of a legitimate marriage' could not succeed to the throne."

"What does Godwineson think he is doing trying to use this fake document? Surely the Court can see through such a tactic!"

"I don't know if such a document is a fake or not, William. Perhaps Abbot Lanfranc can shed some light on it. We had better hope so! The other document is an old letter about the duties involved in giving an oath of fealty. I'll object to it but it isn't really that important one way or another. I have not submitted any list of exhibits on our behalf because, frankly, we don't have anything. We are going to have to rely on the actual testimony of the witnesses, what they saw, heard, did, and the like to establish our case. Live testimony of witnesses will be much more powerful than documents, in any event."

August 20th, 1066
Trial Day 1, Ghent, Flanders

William watched the dawn breaking to what looked to be a beautiful day and thought it an auspicious beginning to the first day of the trial. He and Matilda, and Richard Vos, as well as all their clerks and servants, were staying with Matilda's father, Count Baldwin of Flanders. As the plaintiff's father-in-law, Count Baldwin had recused himself from sitting as one of the possible justices of the court in this matter. The prior evening, the list of the justices who would be sitting on the case had been delivered to the parties. William and Richard had spent several hours going over the names and trying to assess what evidence might persuade each justice and what the general attitude of each might be. William would have preferred to have justices appointed by more dukes and counts and less kings on the panel, but that was not to be. He had tried to persuade his father-in-law not to recuse himself with an argument that since he was the father-in-law to plaintiff and his daughter was sister-in-law to the defendant, he was related to both plaintiff and defendant and therefore could be impartial. However, Baldwin had not been impressed with the argument, and had declined to qualify as Count of a territory which appointed a justice.

Arriving with Richard Vos at court after Mass and breaking their fast, William glanced about the courtroom. Turning to Richard, he said, "This is a very impressive courtroom; entirely suitable to determine the fate of England's king."

As they settled their papers and notes at counsel table, William was looking forward to putting faces to the names of the justices on his list. A few of the justices were personally known to him, but most were not.

Harold and Leofwine had also entered the courtroom and were proceeding to get their documents organized at defendant's table on the other side of the aisle.

William had not seen Harold since he had set him aboard ship to England after Harold pledged his fealty almost two years earlier. He was pleased to see that Harold appeared to have aged in those two years. William thought, *too much negotiation instead of action ages a man!*

The parties had just enough time to get settled when the court bailiff entered his staff striking the traditional blows on the floor as he called the triple "Oyez" to bring the court to order. The fate of England was about to be decided.

Chief Justice Di Vinci appointed by Domenico Di Vinci, Doge of the Republic of Venice, introduced the presiding justices.

After administering the oath to judge fairly in the matter now before the panel of justices, Chief Justice Di Vinci announced that with the consent of counsel, opening statements would not be given. In recognition of the extensive statements filed by the parties at the commencement of the suit, the justices believed that each party's position had been sufficiently set forth. However, each party would be granted the opportunity to submit a closing argument at the close of testimony. Chief Justice Di Vinci then asked if the plaintiff was ready to proceed.

"We are, Your Honor," replied Vicomte Vos.

"Call your first witness, if you would, Counsel," requested the Court.

Vos motioned to William's half-brother, Robert, Comte de Mortain, to come forward and take the witness stand.

Robert arose from where he had been seated and with a slightly hesitant stride, approached to be sworn. The Clerk of the Court stood before the witness stand and administered the oath to Robert. The trial had begun!

Sitting at the back of the courtroom on this first day of the drama that would determine my uncle's future, I watched Robert hesitantly take the stand. He had been kind to me while I was in Normandy, but I thought him a mere shadow of his half-brother. He took the oath to testify truthfully with a weak and wavering voice.

As his testimony went on, he became more confident and his voice strengthened. However, it was obvious that he was not truly comfortable as a witness. I wondered what point Vos intended to make with Robert. Somehow I didn't think it could be of much value coming from such an insipid witness.

In a tone calculated to put the witness at ease, Richard Vos asked, "Would you please state your name and position?"

"Robert, Comte de Mortain."

"Are you related to the plaintiff, Duke William?"

Robert had not expected Vos to ask that question, and for a moment, wasn't sure that the familial relationship should be admitted. He therefore, somewhat hesitantly and apologetically answered, "Yes, He is my half-brother. We have the same mother, but different fathers."

"Now Comte Robert, turning your attention to late fall1064, were you present in Bonneville-sur-Touques at the time that Harold, Earl of Wessex took ship for England?"

"Yes, I was."

"Would you describe what took place, if anything, just prior to Earl Harold and his men going aboard ship for England?"

Vicomte Vos carefully directed Comte Robert's testimony to describe the scene of the oath-taking at Bonneville-sur-Touques. Robert told of the feast and the altar and covered chest which were set up near William. He testified that he heard Duke William tell Earl Harold that he was to swear an oath of fealty to him."

Vos asked, "Did you hear Earl Harold's reply?"

Robert answered he had. "At first, he didn't say anything. He just looked around at his men and his nephew Harkon. Then Duke William said something about since he had just knighted Earl Harold, it was appropriate that he swear an oath of fealty to him."

"What did Earl Harold do or say then, if anything?"

"After a bit of hesitation, he stepped forward and at Duke William's direction, placed his hands on the altar and a chest and swore the oath."

Vos focusing the Court's attention to the words of the oath asked, "what did you hear Earl Harold swear?"

"I heard him swear what sounded like a traditional oath, that he would be faithful to Duke William, that he would support his causes, and that he would do him no harm." Robert sounded more sure of his testimony now.

Vos asked, "When you heard these words, did you believe them to be unusual or different in any way from other oaths of fealty you have witnessed?"

"No, it seemed to be the usual oath sworn to Duke William."

"To your knowledge, was it the same oath taken by others to Duke William when you were present?"

"Yes, it was."

"Have you taken an oath of fealty to Duke William?"

"Yes, I have."

"Was the oath that you swore to Duke William the same oath you heard Earl Harold take?"

"Yes, it seemed to be."

"What happened after Earl Harold swore the oath, if anything?" inquired Vos.

"Duke William embraced him and then Earl Harold, Harkon and his men boarded the boat to return to England." "Thank you, Comte Robert. I have no further questions of this witness, Your Honors."

As Robert of Mortain started to leave the witness stand, clearly relieved this ordeal was over, Harkon thought, *Well, as I expected, that testimony added a whole lot of nothing to Vos's case. Robert is a nice guy but such a wimp! But I guess Vos does have to establish the fact that an oath of fealty was sworn to William.*

Robert of Mortain's evident relief was short-lived, however, as Leofwine Godwineson rose and moved forward to examine the witness. The Court reminded Robert that he could not yet leave the witness stand and that he remained under oath to answer Earl Godwineson's questions truthfully.

Leofwine approached the witness casually and in a tone of easy conversation, said, "Good morning Comte. I won't detain you long, but there are just a few points of your testimony I would like you to clarify." Robert, in his anxiety, had forgotten about t cross-examination. Now he was thrown off guard by the friendly tone and approach of Earl Leofwine.

"Comte Robert, you testified that you also had taken an oath of fealty to your half-brother William, as your overlord, the Duke of Normandy, is that correct?"

"Yes."

"And on that occasion, you were invested with the lands of Mortain, as Comte, to administer on behalf of Duke William, isn't that true?"

"Yes."

"You also received the incomes from the Mortain lands as your personal income, didn't you? You then had an obligation to Duke William to support him in performing his duties as duke by providing men and arms if needed, isn't that true?"

"Yes."

At this point, Robert had started to be less apprehensive of Earl Leofwine's questions, responding to the easy and calm manner in which Leofwine was questioning him.

"So it would be fair to say then that you understood your oath of fealty to be basically an agreement, a contract, between you and Duke William: you received lands and income and in return agreed to administer the lands on behalf of Duke William and, with men and arms, support his causes, isn't that so?"

Before the witness could respond, Vicomte Vos interrupted. "Objection, Your Honor. The witness is not qualified to testify regarding the legality of a contract."

"Your Honor, the witness was asked for his understanding of the agreement or contract, not if was a legally correct one, "argued Earl Godwineson.

After a brief consultation among the justices, the witness was instructed by the Court that he could answer the question, and asked the court stenographer to read back the question posed by Earl Godwineson.

"Ah, yes," finally answered the witness.

"And wouldn't it also be fair to say that, if you were threatened by a revolt or an intruder into your Mortain lands, you understood that you could call upon Duke William to come to your aid, to help you put down any such threats?"

"Yes."

Leofwine had the witness establish that he had paid homage to William and was his vassal. Robert did not fully understand where this questioning was going but intuitively understood that it wasn't a good place. He reluctantly admitted that Harold had not done homage to Duke William.

"In other words, King Harold didn't kneel before Duke William as a vassal, at the time of the oath-taking did he?"

"No."

"In fact, King Harold stood before Duke William as the equal he was, when he gave his oath of allegiance to the Duke, didn't he?"

"Yes."

"So it would be fair to say there was nothing about the ceremony at Bonneville-sur-Touques that would indicate Duke William was King Harold's overlord, that he was the leader and King Harold a lower ranking vassal, wouldn't it?"

"Uh, I guess so," muttered Robert, clearly unhappy at having to answer at all.

Leofwine, with steel in his voice, asked, "Now, you said that you were close enough to Duke William and King Harold to hear most, if not all, of any conversation between them. Other than to direct the defendant to take the oath and where to place his hands, did Duke William have any other conversation with King Harold at that time?"

Startled by the change in tone, Robert hesitated and stumbled with his answer. "I didn't hear any more conversation between them until they took their leave of each other."

"I have no further questions of this witness, Your Honors."

"Redirect, Vicomte Vos?" asked the chief justice.

"Yes, Your Honor." Turning to the witness, Vos asked, "Comte Robert, were you privy to all of Duke William's business affairs?"

"Absolutely not. My brother took counsel when he asked for it but basically ruled the duchy according to his own decisions."

"At any time since you observed the oath of fealty given to Duke William, did you know of or learn of any benefits or honors or lands promised to Earl Harold?"

"After Harold usurped the throne—"

Shooting to his feet, Earl Leofwine said, "Objection, Your Honor, use of the term 'usurped' is biased, inflammatory and a conclusion of law yet to be proven."

Addressing the witness, Chief Justice Di Vinci ordered, "The witness will rephrase his response."

Vicomte Vos turned to Comte Robert, "Please continue, Comte, with what you were saying about when, if at any time, you learned of benefits bestowed upon the defendant by Duke William."

"After my brother learned that Earl Harold had become king, he told me he had intended to protect Harold in his titles and lands when he, William, became king."

"No further questions, Your Honors," said Vos.

"Earl Leofwine?" inquired the Court.

"No further questions, Your Honor."

"The witness is excused," ordered the chief justice. "This Court will reconvene this afternoon at two o'clock."

All rose as the justices exited the high bench.

Vicomte Vos and William left the courtroom heading for William's quarters at the castle. As soon as they were out of hearing of any others, William turned to Richard Vos. "Well, did Robert's testimony hurt us in any way?"

"It's hard to say," Vos responded. "In some of the Justice's countries, an oath of fealty isn't viewed as a contract, so they won't care whether you granted any lands or titles to Harold. But most likely those are also the countries where the oath isn't taken as seriously nor is it as binding, so they probably don't view a breach of the oath as a terribly serious matter. It is not unusual for a person to be required to repeat his oath of loyalty to a lord if there is any suspicion that his loyalty might be wavering.

"For those justices who view an oath of fealty as a contract, with obligations on both sides, they may be beginning to doubt the validity of it, even though sworn on holy relics.

Anyway, let's go eat so we can discuss with Abbot Lanfranc his testimony during dinner and then return to court on time.

Harold and Leofwine, who had been joined by Harkon, watched Duke William and his counsel leave the courtroom, before also leaving for their lodging and dinner.

"I wonder if William realizes just how much his carefully constructed tale has started to unravel," said Leofwine. "I'm sure Vos does, but I bet he doesn't dare tell William how badly Mortain's testimony may have hurt his case. An oath sworn on relics is a serious thing, but without reciprocity of obligations and responsibilities it doesn't mean much. And I think that most of the justices will see it that way."

"Who will Vos call next?" queried Harold.

"Leofwine thought for a moment, and replied, "I think he will likely call Abbot Lanfranc, to establish the irrevocability of a *post obitum* gift before he has William testify to it. Calling a churchman to explain a *post obitum* gift in general, would then give him the opportunity to have William fit his version of it into the churchman's definition. Vos really doesn't have anyone else except William to establish his case. Virtually all of William's assertions are founded on his own knowledge, or what he would have us believe is knowledge.

As the entered their lodgings, Harold led the way, saying, "well, in any event we will soon know. In the meantime, I'm hungry, let's go eat."

August 20th, 1066
Afternoon Session

Arriving after the noon meal at the courtroom at the same time as Harold and his brother, Vos and Leofwine exchanged innocuous pleasantries, much to the annoyance of William. His warrior mindset asked no quarter of an enemy and gave none. One did not engage in idle chitchat with an enemy!

Harold, on the other hand, ever the negotiator, took no offence at the exchange. He had complete confidence in Leofwine's plans to destroy William's credibility in the near future.

The bailiff called the court to order. Chief Justice Di Vinci instructed Vos to call his witness. The bailiff went to the doors of the courtroom, opening them and intoning in a sonorous voice, "Abbot Lanfranc is called to the stand. Please come forth immediately."

A scholarly-looking, middle aged monk entered the courtroom, striding confidently to the witness stand, where he took the oath to testify truthfully, given by the Clerk of the Court.

Vicomte Vos addressed him, "My Lord Abbot, would you please state your name, occupation and title for the court?"

"Certainly. "I am Lanfranc of Pavia, son of Hanbald, Abbot of St Stephen Abbey, also known as Abbaye aux Hommes, at Caen."

Vos then set about establishing the credentials of Abbot Lanfranc as an expert witness, noting that the Abbot was well known as a scholar and teacher of cannon and civil Law, had taught at and was the founder and master of the cathedral school at Avranches prior to becoming a monk at Bec Abbey. After three years in seclusion at Bec, a school was opened there and he became one of its leading teachers. He taught primarily logic and dogmatic theology. He further testified that on many occasions he had been asked his opinion on points of cannon law by cardinals at Rome and by the Pope. Similarly, civil jurists had conferred with him regarding disputed aspects of civil laws?"

"Your Honors, the court and the defendant have received copies of a complete summary of the credentials of this witness. I move that he be allowed to testify as an expert witness with regard to cannon and civil law."

"I have no objections, Your Honor," answered Leofwine.

"There being no objection, the court will accept this witness as an expert witness," ruled the Court.

Vicomte Vos continued with his questioning of the witness. "Abbot, drawing your attention to the subject of a *post obitum* gift, is there a generally accepted legal meaning or definition of the term gift?"

"Yes, there is."

"Would you define the generally accepted legal meaning of that term for the Court?"

"It is generally accepted that the definition of a gift is that it is the voluntary transfer of property or a right to another made without consideration."

"What about a *post obitum* gift, is there is difference between that kind of a gift and a gift in general, such as you have defined?" asked Vos.

Ignoring his role as a witness and assuming the mantle of scholar/teacher, Lanfranc solemnly opined, "A *post obitum* gift is a transfer of property or right(s) wherein the donor (the one making the gift) reserves for himself a life interest in the property with eventual reversion of the property or right upon the death of the donor, to the recipient."

"Are gifts in general, considered to be revocable? asked Vos.

"No. The law usually considers gifts absolute and irrevocable. The law needs a good reason to deviate from the standard and interfere with the presumed irrevocability of gifts."

"If a person made a gift of the right to be his heir, the right to succeed him in his position and title upon his death, what kind of a gift would that be?" asked Vos.

"It would be a *post obitum* gift since the donor would be retaining his position and title during his lifetime and only upon his death would the title and position revert to the recipient."

"And in your expert opinion, would such a *post obitum* gift be revocable?"

"No, it would not," answered Lanfranc to Vos, but also addressing the justices as if they were his first year students at the monastery. "*Inter vivos* gifts—that is the voluntary transfer of property (or rights) by one living person to another living person without valuable consideration upon the condition that the property or right—will belong to the donee, which is perfected, becomes absolute, during the lifetime of the parties. *Inter vivos* gifts are absolute and in order to be valid, they must be irrevocable."

Vos said to the witness, "Thank you for your expert testimony Abbot," and then addressing the Court said, "I have no further questions of this witness, Your Honors."

Chief Justice Di Vinci, glanced at the clock. "Gentlemen, given the late hour of the day, I think this would be an appropriate place to end today's proceedings. Earl Godwinson, you may start your cross-examination of this witness when we reconvene at ten o'clock tomorrow morning. The Court has some matters that it must deal with earlier in the morning."

August 21st, 1066
Trial Day 2, Ghent, Flanders

Day two of the trial started with gray skies and threat of rain. The parties and counsel, and Abbot Lanfranc returned to the courtroom and took their respective places. Despite the gloom of the weather, Abbot Lanfranc, still very much in his scholar/teacher persona, appeared relaxed and not the least bit concerned that he was about to be cross-examined.

Harold, however, had to struggle to maintain a calm, confident demeanor. The weight to be given by the justices to the issue of the irrevocability of Edward's alleged gift would be critical to the outcome of the trial. That thought weighed heavily on Harold. He was relying on Leofwine to undermine Abbot Lanfranc's direct testimony during the coming cross-examination.

Abbot Lanfranc entered the witness box, the Court reminding him he remained under oath. "You may inquire, Earl Godwinson," intoned the chief justice.

"Good afternoon, Abbot. If I recall correctly, previously you said that an *inter vivos* gift, once made, becomes absolute during the lifetime of the parties. Was that your testimony?"

"Yes, essentially that is what I said," responded Abbot Lanfranc.

"I believe you also included the words 'which is perfected', did you not?"

"Yes, *inter vivos* gifts must be perfected to be binding upon the parties and to be irrevocable."

"Would you tell the Court what is the meaning of 'to perfect' such a gift," Leofwine asked a tone of voice of a first year novice needing an accurate definition for the next exam.

Donning his professorial hat, Abbot Lanfranc pontificated, "The classical elements of a valid *inter vivos* gift are (1) an intention to give and surrender title to and domination over the property; (2) delivery of the property to the done; and (3) acceptance of the gift by the donee."

"Would the surrender of and delivery of the property or title be immediate?" probed Leofwine.

"Yes," responded Lanfranc. "The donor merely retains a life interest in the property or title. Upon the making of the gift, the property or title belongs to the donee as of the time of the giving."

"It would also be true, would it not, that the donor would have to have legal ownership of the property or the right to dispose of the title, in order to make the gift of that property or title valid?" inquired Leofwine.

"Yes, that would be true."

"Would any outward sign of the transfer or property or title be required, when such a gift was made?" continued the Earl.

Beginning to understand where the line of questioning was leading, and not happy with where it might end, Abbot Lanfranc hesitated, trying to choose words with the least adverse impact to William's position. He finally responded, "Well, generally, a deed or perhaps even a piece of sod would be exchanged to indicate the transfer of the property. It's difficult to say exactly because there are so many different circumstances."

"In the case of the gift of a title, wouldn't it be necessary that, in the first instance, the devolution or inheritance of the title was within the right of the donor to gift?"

"Yes."

"And wouldn't it be fair to say that there would be some kind of a ceremony of investiture of the donee in the title, in recognition of the gift?"

"Well, there might be an anointing or some other visible sign of the investiture and oaths of fealty and homage given to the donee," replied Lanfranc, attempting to imply that such was not always, or even usually, the case.

"Isn't it fair to say, Lord Abbot, that all three elements of intent, delivery, and acceptance are necessary for the gift to be 'perfected'?"

"Yes, the three elements must be performed to perfect the gift," the Abbot reluctantly agreed.

"Abbot Lanfranc, must the donee be present with the donor for there to be delivery of the gift?"

Automatically assuming his teacher's mantle again, Abbot Lanfranc answered, "No, not at all. The donee need not be present, but whoever is representing the donee is entrusted with the gift and then must, in turn, transfer the gift to the intended donee."

"What would the representative have to do to transfer the gift to the intended donee?" asked Leofwine, knowing full well the difficulties the Abbot would have in answering the question.

"The representative who had received the gift, would have to observe the laws and customs required for effective delivery, when he, in turn, transferred the gift to the intended donee."

"In other words, there would again have to be some outward manifestation of the transfer of the property or right observed a second time, isn't that correct?"

"Yes, that is correct," unwillingly answered the abbot.

"Isn't it also fair to say, Abbot Lanfranc, that without the perfection of the gift, it becomes merely a pious wish of the donor regarding the future disposition of his property?" asked Leofwine sternly, pinning the Abbot with a penetrating glance.

Abbot Lanfranc was too confident a personage to visibly squirm on the witness stand but he came close to it as he answered "yes" to Leofwine's question.

Leofwine, raising his voice, sternly asked, "And isn't it also true My Lord Abbot, that such a pious wish is not enforceable in law?"

"That is correct, it is not enforceable," admitted Lanfranc.

"And none off the legal rules regarding the irrevocability of gifts apply to such a 'pious gift' do they?" asked Leofwine, in an almost thundering tone of voice.

"That is correct," quietly replied Abbot Lanfranc, having no choice but to answer truthfully.

"I have no further questions of this witness, Your Honor," said Leofwine dismissively. He turned his back on the witness and returned to counsel's table.

"Vicomte?" inquired the Chief Justice.

"Yes, Your Honor, just a few questions," responded Vos. Turning to the witness, he asked, "Abbot Lanfranc, you spoke of the requirement of 'delivery' of the gift. In order for the said gift to be properly delivered, is it required of a gift that is not physical property, that the gift be in writing?"

"No, it is not. Oral delivery is still effective delivery," responded the witness, grateful to have been given a question to which his answer would be supportive of Duke William's position.

"And is the presence of the donee required in order to make an effective post obitum gift?

"No, it is not."

"Thank you, Abbot. I have no further questions of this witness, Your Honor."

After Lanfranc's testimony, court was adjourned for the morning, Leofwine and Harold retired to their lodgings to assess the impacts of the morning's testimony. They also needed to prepare for the testimony of Duke William, whom they assumed would begin his testimony at the start of the afternoon session.

"Do you think Lanfranc hurt us?" inquired Harold.

No, I don't think so," answered Leofwine. "In fact, I think just the opposite. I think that William, assuming he testifies as to how and when Edward made this so-called promise, will have a hard time establishing that there was any real intent to gift the crown or that there was delivery of anything tangible."

"I hope you are right," muttered Harold, "but I still am concerned about William's testimony regarding the oath of fealty. I did swear the d— thing."

"Harold, stop torturing yourself over that! Just because you said the words doesn't mean that you have no right to be King of England. William is having his day in court. He will try to make it sound all sacrilegious, immoral and that you should already be roasting in Hell for not keeping your oath. Our turn will come. I will be able to do some damage on cross-examination, but as we discussed, it will be the Bishop Ealdred and the other witnesses who will make the difference and put the oath in its proper perspective."

August 21st, 1066
Afternoon Session

When the court convened that afternoon, the chief justice directed Vicomte Vos to call his next witness. Vos, turning to counsel table where Duke William sat, said, "I call William, Duke of Normandy to the stand."

Duke William, stood, acknowledged the justices and calmly, very much a man in charge of his own destiny, made his way to the witness box.

Richard Vos wasted no time saying, "Would you please state your name and titles you hold, for the court."

"I am William, Duke of the duchy of Normandy, son of Duke Robert I of Normandy, liegeman of Philippe I, King of France, and rightful heir to the crown of England."

"Objection Your Honor," interrupted Leofwine before Vos could ask another question. I move to strike the witness's claimed identification as 'rightful heir to the crown of England'–that is precisely the issue which the plaintiff must prove in this court of law and not, as yet, an established fact which truthfully identifies the witness."

"Your Honor," responded Vos, "as the recipient of a *post obitum* gift from King Edward as his heir, the Duke has every right to claim the title of heir."

There was a short discussion among the justices before the chief justice announced the court's ruling. "At this time, the Court finds that the objected to identification is indeed premature and orders it stricken from the record."

Richard Vos was clearly not pleased with the decision but had no choice but to continue on with eliciting the background information necessary to provide the framework for William's testimony.

Harkon, seated again at the back of the courtroom, listened with amazement as Vos proceeded with his basic interrogation, leading William skillfully down the path of the years of shelter provided to King Edward while he was in exile; how Edward was like a big brother to William, the connection of Edward's mother being William's great aunt; the similar experiences of turmoil or exile before either Edward or William could truly be said to reign. Vos asked questions about William's childhood with his mother at Falaise, his investiture as duke when his father left on pilgrimage to Jerusalem, and his becoming duke at the age of seven when his father fell ill and died on his way home from Jerusalem.

The fact of William's illegitimacy was glossed over. Harkon marveled at how reasonable Vos made this fairy-tale background appear. After all, it was William's father, not William, who had provided most of the years of support to Edward and his brother, With a twenty-two year age difference between Edward and William, there was very little opportunity for interaction between the two second cousins before Edward left Normandy and became an Aetheling of England's Danish King and then King himself. Certainly not enough time given William's minority for Edward to be a 'big brother' to William while he was in Normandy. Any 'cousinly' connection because of Edward's mother Emma being a Norman was certainly not a point to be dwelled upon. Emma had made it very clear what she thought of her firstborn son when she supported his half-brothers by her second husband, King Cnute, over him as successors to Cnute for the English Crown! Edward reciprocated the ill-feelings of his mother. As soon as he became king, he imprisoned her at her castle and wrested the king's treasury from her by force. While his formative years may have been spent in Normandy and he was comfortable with the Norman culture and customs, he never forgot he was an Englishman of royal Saxon lineage.

Harkon wondered why Leofwine wasn't challenging some of this blatantly exaggerated testimony. His uncle wasn't stupid but it sure appeared that he was, when he didn't challenge Vos on any of it.

Leofwine allowed Vos to continue with his direct examination. He became quietly alert, however, once Vos broached the subject of King Edward's alleged promise that William would be his heir.

Vos began the subject by asking, "After Edward had gained his throne in England, did you ever personally meet with him again?"

"Yes, I did."

"When was that?"

"In late summer of 1051, I was invited to England to meet with my uncle Edward."

"What was the purpose of that trip?"

"Edward wanted to be assured that Normandy would not provide a haven for the Danish and/or Norwegian ships that were again raiding the shores of England."

"What, if anything, did you tell King Edward?"

"I assured him that Normandy would not shelter the raiders."

"During these meetings, was there any discussion about who would be his heir in the event of his death?"

"Not during the actual discussion meetings, but afterwards, privately, Edward spoke with me about this."

"Did he name you as his heir at that time?"

"No, not at that time, but he said he would do so at a later time."

"Did you ever learn that King Edward had named you his heir?"

"Yes, I did."

"When was that?"

"The following year, in the fall of 1052."

"Did King Edward personally tell you that he had named you to be his heir upon his death?"

"No, I learned it from Archbishop Robert of Jumièges."

"When did the Archbishop tell you what Edward had done?"

"In the fall of 1052 when he delivered the Godwine hostages to me."

"What did the Archbishop tell you at that time?"

"Objection, Your Honor, hearsay. Archbishop Robert of Jumièges is unable to be called to substantiate what he is alleged to have said."

Vos , knowing the objection would be upheld, quickly responded by saying, "I'll rephrase, Your Honor."

"Duke William, what did you understand to be the message from King Edward?"

"I understood Edward had promised that I was the heir to the throne of England and would be the next king upon his death, and the Archbishop was delivering Edward's hostages from Godwine into my keeping."

"Did you believe that message?"

"Yes. Of course I believed him," answered William testily. "Why wouldn't I? Edward and I had spoken of it when I was in England, and now he had finally decided. Robert was an archbishop of the church as well as a close friend and counselor of Edward. He was delivering Edward's hostages to me. And it was customary, as Edward well knew, to name an heir, giving him dominion over the land and people, but not to take effect until the death of the designator. The same thing was done by my father when he left for Jerusalem."

"I move to strike the witness's answer as to what was 'customary'. It is non-responsive to the question which had already been answered," interjected Leofwine.

"Allowed," responded the Court. "The witness's answer after 'delivering Edward's hostages to me' shall be stricken from the record."

Vos continued on with his inquiries. "To your knowledge, did any of the earls or prelates agree to Edward's designation of you as his heir?"

"I understood from Archbishop Robert that Earl Godwine of Wessex, Earl Leofric of Northumbria, Earl Siward of Mercia, and Bishop Stigand, as representatives of a Witenagemot, all agreed to accept and support me as their next king upon Edward's death."

"Did Archbishop Robert give you any instructions regarding the hostages he was delivering?"

"No, not instructions really."

"What did you understand to be the purpose of the delivery of the hostages?"

"It was my understanding that they were surety that Earl Godwine would remain loyal to Edward."

"Did you have any communication with King Edward after learning of Edward's designation of you as his heir?"

"No, there was no need to do so. It was a completed gift. Of course I accepted his gift, and I understood that after he died, I would be King."

At this point in the examination, the Chief Justice interrupted, "Vicomte Vos, would I be correct in assuming that you will not finish your direct examination of this witness within another hour or so?"

"Yes Your Honor, that would be correct," replied Vos.

Then, in that case, this seems as reasonable a place as any to stop for the day, as it is growing late, Court will re-convene at nine am tomorrow morning. The witness is excused until then."

August 22d, 1066
Day 3 of Trial, Ghent, Flanders

The showers threatening previously, had arrived by sunrise of the third day of trial. William was not concerned about the remainder of his direct examination, and refused to take the weather as an omen for his coming cross-examination, which he expected would start by the afternoon. He and Vos had reviewed as many possibilities for Godwineson's questions as they could envision. William, with his usual arrogance, felt more than a match for a mere English earl. In his own thoughts, he had already determined that when he was king, Leofwine Godwineson would pay dearly for his cross-examination, whatever it turned out to contain.

The bailiff called the Court to order. Chief Justice Di Vinci instructed Vos to recall his witness.

As William took the stand, he was reminded by the Court that he was still under oath to testify truthfully.

At defendant's table, Harold and Leofwine were paid particular attention to Vos. They anticipated that William's testimony would be directed toward the circumstances of Harold's oath of fealty to William. Leofwine knew he had to pay strict attention to William's version of events for his later cross-examination. Harold, on the other hand was dreaded whatever William might say about the oath and how he would malign his character.

Vos started William's direct examination by eliciting a description of the circumstances whereby the Defendant arrived in Normandy in the spring of 1064. He testified how Harold had been shipwrecked off the coast of Ponthieu and taken prisoner by Guy, Count of Ponthieu. Upon learning of Harold's capture, William had immediately gone to Ponthieu and ordered his vassal, Count Guy, to turn Harold and his men over to Duke William."

As William spoke about receiving the news of Harold's capture by Count Guy, Harkon, sitting at the back of the courtroom, vividly recalled the day that news had arrived. A courier had galloped into the castle at Rouen, requesting that he immediately be taken to the Duke. He recalled that Wulfnoth and he had had no idea what the courier's message was but it had resulted in loud expressions of the duke's displeasure. Although neither Wulfnoth nor he could gain access to the duke's office, when the courier was dismissed from the office, they had followed him to the kitchens. Servants are invisible to people like the Duke and Vos, but usually know everything that is going on.

We soon learned the courier's news. Wulfnoth's brother, my uncle Harold Godwineson, had been captured by William's vassal, Count Guy of Ponthieu, and William was going to demand that Harold be turned over to him. Harold, my uncle and Wulfnoth's brother, were coming to William's castle! Maybe we would get to go home now? I realized now how lucky I was that at least I had been able to return home. Unfortunately, Wulfnoth still remained in Duke William's clutches as a hostage. Did anyone know for what reason?

I stopped reminiscing as Vos asked "Did the defendant then return to England?"

"No, he came to Rouen, Normandy with me as my guest."

"While Harold was your guest, did he assist you in the campaign to raise the siege of Rhiwallen's castle at Dol in Brittany?"

"Yes, he did. In fact, later, he saved the lives of two of my men who were caught in quicksand by physically dragging them to safety."

"After the Brittany campaign, did you give any gifts to the defendant?"

"Yes, when we returned to Bonneville-sur-Touques, I gave him a suit of armor to show my appreciation of his aid in the campaign and the saving of my men. Also, it was so he would be suitably attired when I knighted him and he took his oath of fealty to me."

"Did he accept the gift and take an oath to you at that time?"

"Yes, he did. My comtes and vicomtes and vassals who were present saw Earl Harold, swear on holy relics, the oath of fealty to be loyal to me."

"Would you describe how this oath was taken?"

"Earl Harold stood before me, bareheaded and without weapons, and with his hand upon a casket of holy relics and upon the Bible on an altar, made his oath of fealty to me with my court assembled around us to observe it all."

"What did Harold swear to?"

"He swore the customary oath, that he would not injure me, that he would keep my secrets and my castles secure, maintain my judicial rights and all my possessions, and not hinder me in the fulfillment of any of my plans."

"Did you tell Harold that you had been promised you were the heir to King Edward?"

"No, I did not."

"Was there any particular reason why you did not speak of Edward's promise to the defendant?"

"There wasn't any need to. Edward was in good health as far as I knew. I expected that when the time came that Edward died, the promise would take effect and Harold would be loyal and true to his oath and support my claim to the throne."

"What, if anything, happened after the ceremony?"

"Earl Harold, with his nephew Harkon and his men, boarded the ship I had provided and left for England."

"Was the defendant the one to inform you of King Edward's death?" asked Vos.

"No, one of the Norman thanes living in England sent a messenger to me, informing me of Edward's death and the defendant's usurpation of the throne."

"Objection, Your Honor," interrupted Leofwine, rising to his feet. "I move to strike the witness's answer after 'informing me of Edward's death' as non-responsive to the question, prejudicial and hearsay."

"Allowed," responded Chief Justice.

"Did the defendant ever give you any reason for violating his sworn oath to support you and your goals?"

"No, I never heard anything directly from him, just from my informants that he had usurped."

"Leofwine shot to his feet once again. "Objection, Your Honor. Move to strike the witness's answer regarding what he heard from his informants, as non-responsive to the question, hearsay and likely prejudicial."

William showed his annoyance at the interruption while he was answering Vos's question in the way that he wanted it to be answered. He certainly was not accustomed to being interrupted or challenged when he was speaking. In addition, he had not been able to clearly assert his version of events.

Knowing that if he continued with this subject, he would be unable to control William's rising temper, Vos changed the focus of his questions. He hoped that by asking questions concerning his allegations of fraud by Harold, he would give William a legitimate opportunity to vent some of his escalating anger. Vos continued, "Duke William, did you believe that when the defendant swore his oath of fealty to you, that he honestly meant it?"

"Yes, of course I did. He had his hand on holy relics and a Bible when he did so."

"Do you believe at this time, that the defendant honestly meant to be true to you?"

"No, I now know that he never intended to keep his oath."

"What acts or omissions, if any, by the defendant have caused you to believe he never intended to be loyal to you?"

"It is my understanding that he never made any effort at all to support me as heir upon King Edward's death. He made no argument to the Witan regarding my legitimate claim. And he took the throne for himself, knowing he was ineligible since he was foresworn."

"Duke William, is it your belief that King Edward was forced to select the defendant as his heir as he lay dying?"

"Yes, it is."

"On what do you base this belief?"

"During the latter years of King Edward's life, he became more scholarly and religious. He would not have endangered his soul by going back on his prior irrevocable gift unless he had been forced to do so. The defendant was the most powerful man in the kingdom, second only to King Edward. It is my belief that as he lay infirmed and dying, King Edward was in no position to oppose the will of the defendant. He had to do what the defendant ordered him to do."

At this point, Vos thanked the witness for his testimony, and turned to the Court. "Your Honors, I have no further questions at this time, for this witness.

The chief justice glanced at the courtroom clock, and then his fellow jurists. "In that event, Court will adjourn for the morning and resume this afternoon at two."

Walking back to their lodgings, Harold said to his brother, "Correct me if I'm wrong, but that didn't seem to me to be a very compelling case in chief that Vos put on. Did it to you?"

"I agree, but Vos doesn't have much to work with. If Archbishop Robert of Jumièges were still alive, he would have had a lot more factual testimony toward a solid case. Even if the fathers of the northern English earls were alive, they might have been anti-Godwine enough to testify truthfully if they had ever given such assent as William testified to. But even if they had left a record of such an agreement, which they didn't, it would present a problem for Vos since the assent of the Witen has to be given at the time that the Aetheling is about to be crowned, not at some time in the past by a person no longer alive."

"So what happens this afternoon?" Harold asked.

"Well, it should be interesting, to say the least," replied Leofwine. "I'll start the cross-examination of William. Given his temper, I'm hoping I can quickly get him riled enough that he won't be as cautious as he usually is with his responses. You noticed how careful Vos was to avoid any issue of being a bastard, which William is usually pretty sensitive about. He also ignored any reference to Lanfranc's testimony regarding "perfecting" a gift. I'm sure he would like me to avoid that issue as well, but I'm afraid he isn't going to get his wish. Anyway, let's get something to eat—it's going to be a long afternoon."

Harkon joined them as they sat to eat. Once their food and drink had been served, Harkon broached the subject of Leofwine's lack of objections to so much of William's direct testimony. "How could you let William say all those lies and half-truths, Leofwine? Why didn't you object more?"

"You have to remember, Harkon, I am limited on cross-examination to the testimony and issues raised in the direct exam. The more leeway I gave Vos to open new subjects, the wider the scope of my cross-exam can be. I want to be able to challenge William on every little point. To do this, I had to let

Vos open as many doors as I could, so I can slam them shut on cross."

"Well, you sure have your work cut out for you. It's hard to know even where to begin, there's so much that is untrue in his testimony," said Harkon.

"Fortunately, in addition to the cross-examination of William, we also have some pretty strong witnesses for our defense. I think they will strongly impress the justices," replied Leofwine, "but it's still going to be a long next few days, with a lot to be accomplished."

Harkon thought back to their strategy sessions during William's direct examination. Leofwine had explained two major flaws in William's argument for a *post obitum* gift that could be devastating if handled correctly. *I haven't had a chance as yet to see Leofwine in action. Can he pull it off? Is he capable of exploiting either of these flaws? If he can, William will be hoist with his own petard.*

August 22d, 1066
Afternoon Session, Ghent, Flanders

The Court entered the courtroom promptly at two o'clock. Addressing Earl Godwineson, the Chief Justice said, "I believe that the witness is yours to be cross-examined, Counsel, and Duke William, please remember you are still under oath. You may proceed."

As Leofwine rose from counsel table, he made a point of tidying his papers but leaving them in a neat pile. He was betting it wouldn't hurt to seem to have so little regard for cross-examining William that there was no need to refer to notes. And, knowing William truly had no respect or regard for the English as people, even as he professed his right to be their king, anything that he could do to indicate his disdain for him and his claims just might trigger that infamous temper. *Who knows what that might produce*, he thought. *William in his arrogant, calculating, persona was a formidable opponent. William in a rage, while awesome, was a different story.*

"Duke William, since we have not yet had the opportunity to be formerly introduced, let me introduce myself. I am Leofwine, Godwineson, Earl of Essex and Kent, counsel and brother to the defendant King Harold, uncle to your former hostage Harkon Sweinson, and brother to your still-retained hostage Wulfnoth Godwineson."

As he made his introduction, Leofwine was delighted to see a tightening of Duke William's features as he sought to control his response to the mention of Harkon and Wulfnoth

131

Godwineson. "Duke William, directing your attention to the so-called promise of the deceased King Edward about which you have testified, am I correct in understanding that it is your testimony that by this promise, which you call a *post obitum* gift, you would succeed King Edward as his heir to the throne of England upon his death?"

"Yes, that was my testimony."

"And am I correct in understanding that you believe this alleged promise to be irrevocable?"

With his temper wearing a bit thin around the edges at the continued use of "alleged promise", William answered, "There was nothing 'alleged' about the promise! It was made to me and yes, a *post obitum* gift is irrevocable. It is the same as my father's *post obitum* gift of Normandy to me."

"But you were the current Duke, your father's, son, albeit a bastard, were you not?"

"Objection Your Honor," interrupted Vicomte Vos, springing to his feet and giving William a chance to get control of his rising temper. "There is no need for Counsel to insult the witness. I move to strike his characterization and slander of the Duke as 'bastard'."

"Your Honor, I apologize for any insult perceived, such was not intended. However, it is well known fact and a matter of law that the Duke's father was not married to the Duke's mother and thus the termed referred to is legally correct and I respectfully submit not subject to being stricken."

A brief conference was held among the justices before the Chief Justice determined Vicomte Vos's objection overruled.

Having successfully placed William in a position wherein he had to concentrate to control his temper as well as answer questions, Leofwine continued, "My Lord, you were not present when this *post obitum* gift was given to you, isn't that true?"

"Yes."

"And isn't it a fact that you only learned of it when Archbishop Robert of Jumièges came to Normandy to tell you of it?"

"Yes."

"You didn't receive any deed or deeds of lands from Edward from the Archbishop at the time he told you of this gift, did you?

"No."

"Nor did you receive any other documents from King Edward or the Archbishop which would support this irrevocable gift to you, did you?"

"No, I didn't. There was no need of such documents. Edward's royal word was his irrevocable promise!" retorted William.

"So, in fact, the only evidence of this 'gift' was the report of the Archbishop. He merely told you that such a promise had been made, isn't that correct?"

"Yes, but I had an archbishop's word that it was so."

"And you didn't doubt, even a little, that what the Archbishop said, might not be true?"

"No, I did not. After all, he was an Archbishop, a servant of God. He would not lie."

"Yet, he had been outlawed by the English Witenagermot, hadn't he?"

"I don't know."

"But, he never returned to return to his See at Canterbury, did he?"

"In fact, the Archbishop never returned to England after he arrived in Normandy with the hostages, did he?"

At this point before William could answer, Vos stood. "Your Honor, I object to this line of questioning as it relates to the Archbishop's actions and travel, and request that it be stricken as not relevant to the issue at hand. The archbishop is not on trial here."

Leofwine responded quickly. "Your Honor, the witness on direct and on cross-examination had put the credibility and the reputation for truthfulness of the Archbishop into evidence. The veracity of the Archbishop is very relevant to the issue of the alleged promise by King Edward."

Chief Justice Di Vinci said,"The Court will take a recess to discuss a ruling. We will resume testimony in thirty minutes."

Vos met William as he left the witness stand and suggested they get some fresh air. They made their way outside. Vos used this unexpected break to assure William that he was handling the cross-examination well, and to continue to maintain his calm and poise. He reminded him that Godwineson still had a great deal of ground to cover so he would be on the witness stand for a while yet, possibly even another day or so.

"What is Godwineson trying to accomplish with all this nonsense about Archbishop Robert?" queried William.

"He is trying to 'muddy the waters' regarding whether Robert was telling the truth that Edward gave him the message to deliver to you. If he can get the Court to doubt the Archbishop's integrity and truthfulness, it will cast doubt that Edward made the gift, that perhaps it was something that Robert made up for his own purposes."

"What do you think are his chances for accomplishing that?"

"I don't think Godwineson has much of a chance with that argument. After all, Robert was an ordained archbishop, which carries a great deal of prestige, and it's debatable that he would have a private agenda that would suit his purpose to make up such a story. I don't believe the justices will give any weight to a theory that he made up the story for his own purposes. It might make some sort of sense if Edward had been ailing or close to dying at that time. Then, there might have been some private advantage to Robert by such a tale. But that wasn't the case. Edward lived another twelve years. So, to answer your question, I don't think that they will doubt the Archbishop's words.

"In the meantime, just keep calm, answer only the exact question asked. Don't volunteer. Keep your temper. Just remember, Godwineson will try to make you think it's personal, but it's not. He is just doing his job."

Leofwine and Harold had remained in the courtroom, conferring quietly about the direction the cross-examination had been taking and where it should go from this point. Leofwine reviewed his notes for his cross-examination to be certain he had developed all the arguments that would expose William's version of the circumstances for the fabrications that they were.

Harold was curious as to what could be expected from the Court's sudden decision to conference and recess.

"My guess would be that they are concerned with the possibility of maligning an archbishop in open court. But I also think that their ruling doesn't matter very much at this point," Leofwine stated. "They have heard the testimony. Even if they rule it irrelevant, which is likely, that being the politically correct thing to do, they still have received the information. It is much harder to wipe information out of your mind and memory than it is to expunge from the record. In theory, if they rule it irrelevant, the information of his being outlawed has never been said. But as a practical matter, everyone is aware of the fact, which does not reflect well on the Archbishop."

Just then the bailiff announced that the Court was coming in. Vos and William returned to the courtroom: Vos to counsel table, William reluctantly to the witness stand.

When the Court settled into their seats, Chief Justice Di Vinci delivered the ruling on behalf of the Court. "After considerable deliberation, the Court finds that the objection of the plaintiff is sustained, and the challenged testimony will be stricken from the record. You may continue with your cross-examination, Earl Godwineson."

Leofwine, noticing the slight air of superiority on the Duke's expression as he tried to refrain from openly gloating at the decision in his favor, thought, *We'll see just how long that attitude lasts!*

"Duke William, just to refresh our memory after the recess, what year was it that you were advised that King Edward had made this alleged *post obitum* gift to you?"

"1052."

"How old was King Edward at that time?"

"I am not certain.

"Well as a 'close cousin' of King Edward, who you testified was like an older brother to you, surely you know approximately how old he was?"

Leofwine had put the follow-up question in such a way that if he didn't know Edward's age, it would confirm the he really wasn't very close to Edward or he would have to answer the question. Either option was a poor one for William, but after a pause, he finally admitted "I believe Edward was about 47 years old."

"And approximately how old was Queen Edith in 1052?"

"Again, I'm not certain. I met her when I was in England. She was certainly a great deal younger than Edward. I believe she was about 25-26 years old."

"Now, given the ages of this king and queen in 1052, isn't it possible, even likely, that a child, or several children even, might yet be born to this royal couple?"

"I suppose so," answered the Duke reluctantly.

"Yet, according to your testimony, if you were already the king, subject only to the extinction of the life estate by the death of Edward, any child born to this marriage after 1052 would not—could not—become king, isn't that correct?"

William was silent while he tried to produce an acceptable answer to the question, knowing all the while there was no way to answer that wouldn't be damning to him. "No, that's not correct. His son would succeed him. The gift was to have effect only in the event that King Edward died without having sired a son."

"Let me see if I understand your testimony correctly: you became king at the time of the so-called gift of the title, subject only to the death of King Edward. But, if between the time you received the gift which transferred to you all King Edward's rights, and the death of Edward, a son was born to King Edward and Queen Edith, then, even though Edward had died, which should then enable you to fully claim all the rights previously transferred to you, you still wouldn't be the king. Is that your testimony?"

"But a son was not born to them, so I am the king," snarled William.

"Your Honor, please direct the witness to answer the question asked. A simple yes or no answer is all that is required," he added.

"The witness will answer the question," intoned the Chief Justice.

William muttered a barely audible "yes" to Leofwine's question.

"So, the gift of the kingdom would be effectively revoked and Edward's son would be his heir and successor, isn't that true, Duke William?"

"A son of his blood would be his heir, yes," admitted William, trying desperately to avoid mentioning anything about a revocation.

"Duke William, you were in the courtroom when Abbot Lanfranc testified, were you not?"

"Yes, I was," answered William, somewhat surprised at what appeared to be a change in direction of the questions.

"So, you heard his expert testimony that a *post obitum* gift is irrevocable, didn't you?"

"Yes, of course I did," responded William as if Leofwine were an imbecile for even asking the question.

"And isn't it true that you also have testified that you believe a *post obitum* gift is irrevocable?"

"Yes, because it is."

"Then, Duke William, if the alleged gift to you by King Edward is revocable upon the birth of a son between the time of the gift to you and the end of the life estate held by King Edward, the alleged gift cannot be a *post obitum* gift, can it?"

Duke William's flushed face and threatening scowl showed more clearly than words che had just realized the box he had been put in, albeit too late to avoid. He tried to dodge an answer by claiming ignorance of the law, that he wasn't a clerk versed in cannon law, but the damage had been done.

Insult was added to injury when Leofwine blatantly ignored his answer and turned to the Court. "My Lord Justices, with your permission I would like to suggest that my cross-examination of Duke William be suspended for the day. I have sufficient examination still to conduct that it would not be finished in the next several hours."

Chief Justice turned to Vicomte Vos. "Have you any objections Counsel?

"No, Your Honor," said Vos, only too glad to have been given the opportunity to get William off the witness stand before he said or did anything irreparable.

"Then we stand adjourned until nine a.m."

As Leofwine prepared to leave the courtroom, slowly gathering his papers, he cautioned Harold to keep a calm demeanor and avoid even looking at William. The Duke was a powerful man and when embarrassed as he had just been, was not someone to further goad.

Vos ushered the Duke out of the courtroom as quickly as he could. Leofwine dallied at counsel table long enough to avoid leaving at the same time. Harold and Leofwine waited while Harkon joined them from his seat at the rear of the courtroom. With a smile on his face, Harkon congratulated Leofwine. "That was very nicely done, Uncle! If William had been armed, you would have come very close to being run through," he said with a laugh. "I'm glad we aren't quartered anywhere near him. It's likely to be very noisy around William tonight."

Harkon was truly impressed with the way that Leofwine conducted the cross-examination. He had come to know and like his uncle in the two years that he had been home, but he hadn't been convinced that he was up to the job of defending the king in this trial. Leofwine was loyal to Harold to a fault and a competent warrior but Harkon had wondered if he had that 'killer instinct' to really go after someone as powerful as William. Now he had his answer. Yes, he did!

The rain had stopped, and the clouds had given way to late afternoon sun. The greenery around the courthouse was damp and clean, reflecting the sunlight with a sparkle. The three men took advantage of the pleasant late afternoon weather to clear their heads after the closeness of the courtroom by walking to their lodgings. They refrained from even thinking about the tasks for tomorrow, just enjoying the end of the strain of today.

August 22d, 1066
Count Baldwin's Castle, Ghent, Flanders

At Count Baldwin's castle, the atmosphere was anything but serene. William was in a towering rage, berating Vos in a voice that could be heard in the depths of the kitchens. Vos was attempting to give William some answers and was trying to get William to calm down knowing there was more to come. William had to be brought to a point where he could be coached and prepared for more of Godwineson's cross-examination coming in the morning.

"Richard, how could you let this happen?" raged William. "He made me look like an idiot! Are you going to let this happen again, tomorrow? You had better not! I will not be toyed with like that." He rampaged about the chamber, each stride landing as if he were squashing a bug beneath his foot.

"William, unless you had lied under oath, there was nothing that could have been done once Godwineson raised the issue of a potential child of Edward. You know he named you his heir only in the event he died childless, which he did, but still, there was that condition. There was no condition when your father had you invested as duke while he was still alive. Now forget today. It's over. We have to prepare for tomorrow, which is going to be just as difficult, I'm sure. Godwineson knows what he is doing and you have to be prepared for it."

Begrudgingly, William stopped his pacing, refilled his goblet with wine and sat down. "Alright, you have my attention. What will tomorrow bring? Whatever it is, I doubt I will like it, if today is any indication of what is to come."

"You are probably correct there," answered Vos, with a wan smile, and a sigh of relief that William was finally ready to settle down to a serious discussion. "There are several areas of your direct testimony which Godwineson needs to attack. Since our Complaint has the double-edged sword of counts of foresworn and fraud, and both rest on the oath of fealty, I think that is where he will start. Your job will be to keep reminding the Court that Harold's actions showed that he never intended to have any allegiance to you, that his oath was a fraud to God and to you from the very beginning. It doesn't matter that if he didn't know of the holy relics. He knew of the bible on the altar on which he placed on hand. That was enough to bind an oath. You have to remind the Court of that fact whenever you can."

August 23d, 1066
Day 4 of Trial, Ghent, Flanders

Harkon, Harold and Leofwine had spent the evening reviewing the afternoon's cross examination and discussing its effect on the defense as a whole. Each agreed that William had not come out of it a winner. It was more important than ever that William continue to be angered and rattled. With that goal in mind, they went over in fine detail Leofwine's plan for today's cross. Harkon was pleased that he had been able to contribute his firsthand knowledge of several oaths sworn to Duke William that he had personally observed while he had been held hostage in Normandy. He had heard the actual words spoken as the oath so Leofwine would know if the Duke testified to some other words in Harold's case.

The plan was to show that Harold wasn't a guest; he was a well-treated prisoner. He was not free to leave until and unless William said so. After that, the emphasis would be on the inadequacy of the oath itself, and the threat to Harold, his men and Harkon and Wulfnoth if Harold refused to take the oath.

As he awaited William taking the stand, Harkon mused that while last night's strategy was a sound one, William could be cunning. Leofwine would have to be very careful to keep William's testimony going down the path Leofwine indicated. Granted the Archbishop would testify later about the reciprocity of obligations of an oath, so there would be back-up for the cross-examination of William on the subject. *But,* he thought, *I wouldn't mind seeing William really put on the hot seat at all. Twelve years requires a lot of payback!"*

Now, from his usual seat at the rear of the courtroom, Harkon watched William resume the witness stand at the start of the fourth day of trial. Outwardly, he seemed to be his usual confident self. As usual, he was dressed in simple clothing of expensive materials, and carrying himself as the solder he was. But Harold quietly whispered to Leofwine, and at the same time, Harkon sent a note to Leofwine. Both men, very familiar with William's looks and demeanor, apprised Leofwine of what they had noticed. Namely, that William was showing signs of the strain. He was losing his usual almost ruddy, outdoorsman color. His eyes were more wary than piercing. His body language conveyed an aura of defiance rather than that of his usual confident arrogance.

Leofwine took note of their comments. He stood to address the witness, making no attempt to be the aggressive interrogator of yesterday. "My Lord Duke, I direct your attention to the period of time when King Harold, then Earl of Wessex, was in Normandy in 1064. Recalling your earlier testimony, you testified that you required Count Guy, who was holding King Harold and his men for ransom after they had been ship wrecked at Beaurain, to turn King Harold and his men over to you, isn't that correct?"

"Yes," responded William tersely. He had learning the hard way the hazards of volunteering more than the minimum required.

"And when you arrived at Count Guy's, did you learn that the boat in which the king and his party were sailing had been destroyed when they landed upon Count Guy's shores?"

"Yes, I did."

"When you had King Harold transferred to your custody, what did you consider to be his status?"

"He was my guest! He was the leading Earl of England. What else would he be?"

"So, of course, there would be no question of a ransom being paid, is that correct?"

"Yes, of course it is. I just said he was a guest!"

William was getting annoyed at the simplicity of it and its lack of direct relevance to what he considered important, which was precisely what Leofwine was aiming for. He took a deep breath, and in a casual tone, continued with this non-threatening line of questioning. "So after suitable exchange of thanks and the like, you provided the Defendant with a ship to return home, since, as your guest, King Harold was free to return to England, is that correct?"

William, trying to determine how to answer this unexpected question, finally answered, "Well, more or less, yes."

"Isn't it a fact, Duke William," barked Leofwine in an outraged tone of voice, "that you didn't provide transportation for the Defendant to return to England for four months?"

"It may have been about that long, but there were matters in Normandy that demanded my immediate attention."

Keeping a challenging tone, Leofwine threw out the next question. "Isn't it true, Duke William, that while outwardly treated as a guest, the Defendant was in fact your prisoner, with no freedom to leave Normandy until you allowed it?"

"No, of course he wasn't," replied William indignantly. "As I said, he was my honored guest. I even knighted him for saving two of my men when we were on campaign in Brittany."

"Is it your testimony then, that, rather than return to England after his shipwreck, he freely chose to risk his life and that of his men to join you in a campaign in Brittany, which would benefit solely you and/or Normandy?"

"Yes, he did."

"Isn't it true, Duke William, that the only means that King Harold had to return to England was if you provided a ship for him and his men?"

"Yes, which I did."

"But it took you four long months, didn't it?"

"As I just said," answered William, trying very hard to sound reasonable and not defensive, "there were some emergencies that arose in Normandy which I had to deal with before I could help Harold out, so it was a little while before I could arrange for a boat for him."

"Critical events like your invasion of the neighboring lands of Brittiany, isn't that correct?"

"It wasn't an invasion! Normandy was threatened and needed to be defended."

"And rather than leave King Harold alone in Normandy, or allow him to make his own way back to England while you were gone, he was required to march with you into Brittany and engage in your battle at Dol, isn't that correct?"

"No, it isn't. Earl Harold, in return for my getting him out of a tight spot with Count Guy, chose to support me. In fact, afterwards, I knighted him for his bravery and the fact that he saved two of my men from drowning in quicksand at Mont St. Michel."

"When and where did this knighting ceremony take place?" asked Leofwine.

"After we returned from Brittany, a few weeks before Christmas, a feast was arranged to celebrate the successful campaign at Bonneville-sur-Touques."

"Before King Harold and his men were allowed to go aboard that ship, isn't it true that you required the Defendant to take an oath of fealty to you?"

"I had just knighted him, so of course he would swear an oath of fealty to me," William answered testily.

"Is it customary in Normandy for the one swearing his allegiance to swear such an oath on both an altar and a chest covered so its contents are hidden from the oath-taker?"

"For such an important person as Earl Harold, it was a fitting solemnity."

"Fitting or not, His Highness was unaware that the oath was being sworn on holy relics, wasn't he?"

"No, I wouldn't say that."

"You wouldn't? Well, let me ask you, were the holy relics exposed to everyone's sight?"

"No. The casket they were in was draped with appropriate altar cloths."

"Did you tell His Majesty the contents of the casket upon which he placed his hand?"

"No, there was no need, it was obvious the casket contained special relics, else why place your hand there?" William grew more sarcastic by the moment.

"Well, to answer your question even though I am the one asking the questions," replied Leofwine conversationally, not letting William's sarcasm upset him in the least. "Isn't it true that since this was your ceremony, you ordered him to place his hand on the casket as well as the altar?"

"I told him what the procedure was and what was required by the ceremony, yes."

"So let me summarize your testimony to be sure I understand it. You have just testified that you required King Harold to take an oath of fealty, before embarking on a ship to England. And at your direction, this oath was sworn by him with one hand upon an altar and the other hand upon a covered casket, which contained holy relics, but his Majesty didn't know what the casket contained. Is that your testimony?"

Well..." William started to embark upon an explanation.

"A simple yes or no answer is all that is required Duke William. Please answer the question."

"Yes," replied William, clearly feeling that no one had the right to tell him to stop talking when he had something he wanted to say.

"Duke William, with regard to the actual oath taken by the defendant, what promises did he make, if any, by that oath?"

"Earl Harold swore to be loyal to me, to keep my secrets, maintain all my legal rights and possessions and not hinder me in the fulfillment of any of my plans, all of which he failed to do!"

"My Lord Justices, I move to strike the last part of the witness's answer as unresponsive to the question and the witness's biased opinion of a matter which is for this Honorable Court to determine."

"Objection, Your Honor," responded Vicomte Vos. "The witness was merely answering the question posed by counsel."

After a very brief poling of the Justices, the Chief Justices ruled Leofwine's motion denied.

Earl Leofwine continued, "Was the oath sworn by King Harold essentially the same as that sworn by other comtes and vicomtes of Normandy to you?

"Yes."

"And isn't it true that when your comtes and vicomtes swear their allegiance to you, as their Duke, you grant or have already granted land or other benefices to the recipient's and you in turn, swear to protect them in their holdings and rights?"

"Yes."

"So in exchange for this promise to be loyal and support your legal causes, you are obligated to provide protection to the one who has sworn an oath of fealty to you. Is that correct?"

"Yes."

"But you didn't grant any Norman lands or other benefices to the then Earl of Wessex, did you?

"Yes, I did."

"What did you grant to Earl Harold?

"I promised that when I was King of England, I would protect him in his lands and titles."

"Let me be sure I understand," asked Leofwine, appearing a bit confused. "In 1064, in exchange for his allegiance to you, you promised the Defendant that at some unknown future time when you became King of England, you would protect him in his lands and titles, of which he had already been in possession for years and which, by your oath taken upon being crowned, you had sworn to defend and protect. Is that your testimony?"

"No, that's not what I meant."

"Do you mean you did grant him Norman lands or incomes?" quickly rapped out Leofwine.

"Well, no but..."

"Did you mean you would come to his aid all the way from Normandy and protect him if any of his lands or possessions in England were threatened? Is that what you meant?" Leofine asked, interrupting William's attempt to explain.

"Of course not," responded William.

"You couldn't protect him from any enemies or invasion of his rights, since he wasn't in Normandy, could you?"

William finally lost his temper. "I could and would have protected him when I became king, had he been faithful to me!"

"Then," asked Leofwine conversationally, "until such time as you became king of England, you were in no position to fulfill any obligations to Harold created by his oath of fealty to you in 1064, were you?"

"My obligations were to protect him which I would have done as his king."

"But when would you have fulfilled these obligations under Harold's oath of fealty?"

"I just said, when I became king!" William was almost shouting at Leofwine now.

"But had King Edward lived longer, it might have been years before you had any obligations to the Defendant, isn't that correct?"

"I suppose so."

Leofwine pounced on William's evasive answer. "Duke William, did you not testify that your promise to the Defendant was that when you were king, you would confirm him in his titles and protect his holdings, isn't that what you said?"

"Yes."

"Therefore, it is true, is it not, that it could have been years from 1064 before you were the king and in a position to fulfill your promise to the Defendant?"

As William hesitated once again, Leofwine turned to the Court. "Your Honor, please instruct the witness to answer the question. It requires only a simple yes or no answer."

Faced with this, William had no choice but to respond, "Yes."

"Duke William, at the time of the oath-taking, you granted no protection or benefices to King Harold in Normandy, isn't that true?"

"No, it's not."

"What benefit do you say you provided to the Defendant?"

"I provided a boat for him to return to England with his men."

"So in exchange for his oath to you, you released your prisoner and allowed him to return home, is that your testimony?"

"No its not. Harold wasn't a prisoner; he was a guest."

"In fact, this exchange of obligations created by this oath of fealty was purely a one-sided arrangement wherein King Harold was immediately bound to be loyal to you and strive in your behalf, but you had absolutely no obligations or duties to him until such time as you became king of England, which could have been years from the time of the oath, isn't that so?"

"No, that's twisting my testimony," answered Duke William. "I became king upon Edward's death and Earl Harold had an obligation and duty to support me as his liege lord, not usurp the crown!"

Ignoring William's anger and using an incredulous tone, and an air of innocence, Earl Godwineson, partially addressing the Justices, said, "Duke William, are you telling this Honorable Court that the Defendant was currently sworn to support your goal to become king of England during however many years might pass until King Edward died, and only after the passage of these unknown number of years, would you have any obligations to King Harold, and even then, your only obligation would be to allow him to keep the lands and titles which he has already had for years, and which under your oath as King, you were bound to recognize as lawfully held? Is that your testimony?"

Vos jumped to his feet. "Objection Your Honor."

Before he could articulate his objection, Leofwine said, "I withdraw the question, Your Honor."

"Duke William, you commanded that the Defendant take this oath on hidden relics before he and his company were allowed to embark upon the journey to England, isn't that so?"

"No, that's not the way it was," answered William.

"But even having commanded the taking of the oath, and even though the boat was there, not all of his company was allowed to return to England on this boat, were they?"

"Yes, of course they were," responded a puzzled William.

"Isn't it fact, Duke William, that Wulfnoth, the younger brother of the defendant, was not permitted to return to England with his brother in '64?"

"He did not return to England with Earl Harold."

"And isn't it a fact that Wulfnoth remains to this day, in your custody and control, and has not been allowed to return to England...that to this day he is still kept as a hostage. Aren't those the true facts?" thundered Leofwine in righteous indignation.

William attempted a righteous tone. "He wasn't part of Earl Harold's company. He had nothing to do with Earl Harold returning to England."

"Isn't it true then, by that reasoning, that Harkon Sweinson had 'nothing to do with Earl Harold returning to England'?" asked Leofwine, smoothly.

"I don't know, I suppose so," muttered William.

Pinning the witness with a harsh gaze, Leofwine, stated the obvious. "Yet Harkon Sweinson, who had been in your custody for twelve long years and was clearly not a member of the Defendant's men captured by Count Guy, who later became your 'guest', was allowed to return to England, wasn't he?"

Not liking it one bit but having no choice, William answered, "Yes."

"Duke William, do you or do you not now continue to hold as a hostage Wulfnoth Godwineson, denying him freedom to return to England? Yes or no!"

"Glaring, and daring Leofwine to do anything about it, William answered, "Yes."

At this point, the Chief Justice asked Leofwine if he was nearly finished with his cross-examination of Duke William. Earl Godwineson replied that he was not, that he likely had more than another hour before his cross was finished. In that case, the Chief Justice ordered court adjourned for the noon recess, to reconvene at two o'clock that afternoon.

As the parties headed to their lodgings for the noon meal, Harkon asked Leofwine, "Do you really have that much more to ask the Duke?"

"Not really, but if I can stretch the testimony into the afternoon, then Vos has less time to either try to rehabilitate William or prepare his next witness. I doubt that he is going to try to rescue William's testimony. He has another witness, the Duke's secretary, who I really hope he puts on the stand. If he questions him as I think he is going to, I am hoping to prove this witness's testimony is a double-edged sword, that will likely be of more help to me than to William's case. If he doesn't call him, I have a subpoena ready to serve on him before he can leave the courthouse. I know he is here, just sequestered. Even if he is going to rest his case-in-chief, the Court might be willing to give me leave to start our defense tomorrow morning, instead of late this afternoon."

August 23d, 1066
Afternoon Session

Once the justices had all taken their places, the Chief Justice addressed the parties. "Gentlemen, I believe the Plaintiff is still on the witness stand and remains under oath. Earl Godwineson, you may continue with your cross examination."

Duke William glared at Godwineson as he stood to address the witness. He and Vos had not come up with any answer to the question of the direction or subject of the next round of cross-examination questions.

William had steeled himself for the questions to come, but was visibly aware that from whatever direction or whatever subject, he wouldn't like them.

Casually, almost softly, the Earl asked, "My Lord, in order to give someone a gift, would you believe it necessary for the gift-giver to own the gift he was giving?"

"Yes, of course."

"In other words, the donor, gift-giver would have to have all right, title and interest in and to the subject of the gift, in order to transfer his interest in that gift to another person, is that your understanding?"

"As I already said, yes, of course it would have to be his, for him to give it away," answering in a tone that clearly implied Leofwine was some kind of an idiot for even asking such a question.

"Now, let me ask you, how did your family acquire the lands of Normandy?"

Somewhat taken aback by the seemingly switch of subject, William none the less answered without sarcasm, "Originally, my ancestor Rollo received the lands that are now called Normandy from the King of France."

"Would it be fair to say that your ancestor Rollo became a vassal of the King of France?"

"Yes."

"Would it also be fair to say that Rollo paid homage to the then King of France and swore an oath of fealty to him?"

"Yes."

"The Duke of Normandy, prior to you becoming its duke, was Robert I, your father, was it not?"

"Yes."

"While you were yet a child, your father Duke Robert I decided that he would make a pilgrimage to Jerusalem, is that correct?"

"Yes."

"What action, if any, did your father take regarding the governance of Normandy, prior to leaving the duchy?"

Answering a bit more hesitantly as he began to see where this seemingly wandering questioning was leading, William answered, "He had me invested as his heir, as the Duke of Normandy."

"Would you describe what took place for this investiture?"

"The comtes and vicomtes of Normandy were called to attend my father at Rouen. He told everyone of his plans to go to Jerusalem. He said I was his heir as the successor Duke of Normandy. I was fully invested as Duke of Normandy. All the comtes and vicomtes paid homage to me as my vassals and swore an oath of fealty to me as duke."

"Would it be fair to say that thereafter there were two dukes of Normandy?"

"Yes, I was also the duke but my father retained a life estate as duke and I could not exercise the powers of being the duke until his death."

"And when your father failed to return from Jerusalem, extinguishing his retained life estate, since you were already the Duke of Normandy, you were immediately able to exercise the powers of the duke, weren't you?"

"Yes."

"But in order to complete the process of becoming the undisputed Duke of Normandy, wasn't it necessary that the Duke's overlord, the King of France, approve of the succession?

"Yes."

"Did Henry I King of France approve of you as your father's heir?

"Yes, he did."

"As the new Duke of Normandy, did you pay homage to King Henry I of France as his vassal and swear an oath of fealty to him as your overlord?"

"Yes."

"Was that oath of fealty to King Henry of France, essentially the same oath of fealty that was sworn by King Harold to you?"

"Yes, it was more or less the same."

"Except, of course, in the case of the Defendant, he wasn't also your vassal, was he?"

"No, he wasn't my vassal, he just swore allegiance to me!"

"And he didn't paid homage to you, did he?"

"No, he just swore an oath of allegiance to me."

"And that oath, which was taken to show allegiance and loyalty between equals, contained the language that he, Harold, swore to you, William, to be loyal and true and to support your goals and aims with the exception of the respect and faith that he owed to his king, his sovereign and to his heirs, isn't that correct?"

"No, it did not," stated William, emphatically.

"Was it your intention then, by the omission of this customary phrase, to have Harold's oath to you take precedence over the defendant's prior oath of loyalty to his king?" Leofwine continued.

"No, it just wasn't necessary to include it in the oath Harold was taking."

"Then it would be fair to say that both parties understood that this oath did not take precedence to the oath of fealty swore by each party to their king, of whom each party was a vassal, wouldn't it?"

"Yes."

"Duke William, would you consider it a breach of an oath of fealty if one of your vassals who had also sworn such an oath of fealty to you, were to attack any of your household troops?"

"Yes. Of course it would be a breach of his oath."

"So, when your armed forces attacked your overlord, King Henry of France's forces at Montemer, that was a breach of your oath to your overlord, the King of France, wasn't it?"

"No it was not. I was defending my Duchy lands which were being attacked by King Henry!" thundered William.

"Then is it your testimony that under some circumstances when taking arms against your overlord and one to whom you have sworn allegiance, it is not a breach of an oath of fealty? That the allegiance can be revoked for example, in defense of your lands as you just said? Is that correct?" asked Leofwine.

William once again realized too late that the door of the box had closed behind him with no way out but to admit to Leofwine's question. He hesitated in answering, knowing whichever way he answered would not be to his advantage, but finally muttering a subdued, "Yes."

Turning to the Court Leofwine said, "I have no further questions of this witness Your Honor," and returned to counsel's table.

"Redirect, Vicomte?" inquired the Chief Justice.

"Yes, Your Honor," stated Vos.

Silently praying that even though they hadn't discussed his coming question, William would understand it and respond accordingly, Vos approached the witness. "My Lord, what do you consider to be the primary duty of the Duke of Normandy?"

Almost holding his breath, Vos awaited William's answer.

William paused a moment, giving the question serious thought and answered, "To protect my people and their property."

Inwardly heaving a huge sigh of relief at William's answer, Vos continued with renewed confidence. "At about the time that Defendant's counsel referred to, the altercation at Mortemer with King Henry, did you learn what was happening in and around the lands at Mortemer?"

"Yes, I did."

"What did you learn?"

"I was given reports that King Henry's army was plundering and ravaging the homes and field of my vassals and killing my people."

"What, if any, action did you take in response to those reports?"

"I gathered an armed force and attacked King Henry's forces."

"And you did this knowing that you had taken an oath of fealty to King Henry?"

"Yes, but I had no choice. My duty was to protect the safety of my people, and since Henry had breached his duty to me as his vassal in the first instance, I was not in breach of any oath of fealty to him."

Satisfied that he had rehabilitated William in-so-far as possible, Vos said, "I have no further questions, Your Honor."

"Earl Godwineson, re-cross?" asked Chief Justice.

"Just a few questions to clear up a point, Your Honor."

Addressing Duke William, Leofwine asked, "You testified that King Henry breached his duty to you, did you not?"

"Yes, I did because he had breached it," rebuked William.

"Isn't it true that one of the places where you allege that King Henry attacked, was the castle of Count William of Arques, one of your vassals?"

"Yes."

"As one of your vassals, Count William of Arques was also a sub-vassal of King Henry, isn't that correct?"

"Yes."

"And as a sub-vassal of King Henry, William of Arques had the right to appeal for help from his and your overlord to lift the siege which your forces had in place at his castle at Arques, prior to King Henri's entering Normandy with troops, didn't he?"

"No, he didn't."

"Let me be sure I understand your testimony: you could take up arms against your overlord if he breached his duty to you first, but Count William of Arques was breaching his duty to you by seeking help from his King even though you first had breached your duty to him and laid siege to his castle, is that your testimony?"

"No, that isn't what I meant or said," William snapped.

Leofwine, believing that he had made his point, despite William's denial, told the Court he had no further questions for this witness and sat down.

At this point, the Court addressed counsel. "Gentlemen, the hour grows late and this appears to be a logical place to terminate the testimony for the day. Vicomte Vos, have you further witnesses to present?"

"Yes, Your Honor, there is one more witness to be called."

"Could you give the Court an approximate amount of time you will need for this witness? I ask not to place constraints upon your case but because the Court has other urgent business it must attend to and cannot give but half a day tomorrow to this case."

"I would expect that either the morning session or that of the afternoon, at the Court's convenience, would be ample time for this witness, Your Honor."

"Then court will adjourn for today and reconvene at nine tomorrow morning."

As Harold and Leofwine gathered their papers and left the courtroom, they were joined by Harkon, who was bursting with impatience to ask Leofwine what he thought the Court would make of the information that Wulfnoth was still being held hostage.

"I really don't know," answered Leoffwine. "Most of the court's members are used to exchanges of hostages for various reasons, so they might not think too much about it one way or another. But I had the opportunity to make the point, so I did. I can't say that I had really planned to do so. In closing argument, I can refer to the situation again, especially that the hostages were originally given to secure Godwin's alleged promise to Edward. With Godwine dead these past thirteen or so years, and Edward now dead, there wouldn't appear to be any reason for hostages from anyone. William had to say it was separate from Harold's oath, so it wouldn't seem to be required to ensure that Harold kept his promise of allegiance to William. Plus, since Harold wasn't the one to agree to

Wulfnoth being a hostage, it would certainly smack of coercion of him if his oath was the reason for a hostage."

Arriving at their lodging, the three men agreed to meet for the evening meal, and after they had eaten, spend some time discussing what the morning might bring.

August 23d, 1066
Evening, Ghent, Flanders

William was tired and angry. Even the time spent relaxing from the long court day and having a good meal had not improved his disposition. The only redeeming feature of the day had been a short meeting with his brother Bishop Odo after court had adjourned and while Vos was absent attending to some details for tomorrow. Odo's news was good. He reported that the fleet was nearing completion and there were many volunteers ready and willing to go to war. The main problem was that the winds needed to cross the channel were being contrary. But since they were planning to await the end of the trial and the Court's decision in any event, the winds were not of immediate concern. Further, although it was a large gathering at Dives, it appeared that so far, nobody was questioning the purpose of this gathering of men and boats. There was no indication that the justices of the court were aware of this assembly of men nor of its intended purpose. Even though kings, counts and dukes of their respective territories were allowing their vassals to join in this enterprise, to date, this permission was not deemed noteworthy enough for their justices at court to be informed of it. William fervently hoped the situation would remain that way, at least until the trial ended.

Upon meeting after the meal with Vos, William's first question was a surly, "So who are you putting on the witness stand tomorrow, and will it do any good?

"When we were originally reviewing what would be your testimony, you described your meeting with Archbishop Robert. You didn't make note of it at that time but it occurred to me later that your secretary likely had been present during that meeting. I asked him about it and he said he was present. I am calling him as witness tomorrow to confirm what the Archbishop told you about being the heir. You didn't notice him in the courtroom because he has been sequestered. His testimony will be more effective for not having heard your direct of the subject. But he has been prepared so he is aware of the general gist of your testimony about the meeting, and can confirm that is what he heard also. It shouldn't take long. I don't anticipate that Godwineson will have much if any lengthy cross-examination of him. Then we will have until Monday morning to prepare for Harold's defense."

"That's just as well. I still have a duchy to administer and not much is getting done while I sit here in Ghent."

The Godwinson men, however, were in good spirits. They felt that the cross-examination had gone well so far. While not sure of the exact content of Vos' next witness it was known that he was William's secretary, so it was most likely that he would merely bolster William's version of things, rather than introduce any new bombshells.

Leofwine was particularly pleased that the trial schedule had worked out such that he would have two and a half days to fine tune the presentation of the defense's case-in-chief. It was a lucky break for the defense to have the extra time to review and incorporate any salient points that had been exposed during Vos' case-in-chief.

If they were really lucky, thought Leofwine, whatever business the Court had on Friday afternoon, might not be concluded and run over until Monday, in which case he would have even more time before he had to start the defense. As he and Harold had previously discussed, each day of trial was a benefit to Harold and to William, a day lost of the chance to invade. this season. In the meantime, they all enjoyed a good meal, and a relatively care-free evening, knowing that there was little or no more damage to be done by William's allegations.

August 24th, 1066
Day 5 of Trial, Ghent, Flanders

The morning session of court started promptly at nine o'clock, with the Chief Justice giving permission for Vicomte Vos to call his next witness, Brother John of the Abbey of Saint-Étienne in Caen, Normandy. William had used one of these monks as his personal secretary since founding the Abbey as part of the reconciliation of William and the Pope, after the Pope had forbidden William's marriage to Matilda.

After establishing that Father John was a Benedictine monk of the Abbey, and was chief secretary for Duke William, Vos began the meat of the testimony. "Father John, calling your attention to the day in the fall of 1052 when Archbishop Robert of Jumièges arrived at Duke William's castle in Rouen, do you recall that day?"

"Yes, I do."

"Would you describe the arrival of the Archbishop for the Court?"

"Well, Duke William was expecting him, because an outrider had arrived a bit earlier to warn of the company's arrival. We were about to sit down to eat when they arrived. The outrider had said the Archbishop was arriving but hadn't said anything about the young boys with him. So initially there was some confusion as to arrangements for the boys, but Duchess Matilda with the Duke's squire soon got it straightened out and took charge of the boys. The Archbishop was too tired to meet with the Duke for any serious discussions that evening, so, after eating, he retired."

As Father John testified to the company's arrival at Rouen, Harkon, listening to the testimony from the back of the courtroom, thought back to that evening Father John was so blithely describing. To calmly state that there was 'some confusion' was the understatement of the year! Harkon remembered with acute clarity the terror of that entire trip. He had been scooped up without warning from the new household where he had just recently moved into in order to start learning to be a squire. He had barely gotten settled when he was ordered to gather his things and come to the courtyard to join the Archbishop there. To his surprise, his things were loaded on a cart and he was tossed up in front of one of the mounted men at arms and they left! Nobody thought it worth their while to tell him why they were leaving, where they were going, or anything else, for that matter. After all, whoever explained things to a six-year-old? It wasn't until the troop made its first rest stop that he realized his Uncle Wulfnoth was also in the company, but at sixteen, he was old enough to have been allowed his own horse. Although Wulfnoth was closely guarded, they let him speak to him briefly. Scared, exhausted and still a bit teary-eyed, he tried to conceal it seeing that wherever they were going, Wulfnoth was at least going with him. That had given him some degree of comfort at the time. It remained a trip indelibly engraved in vivid detail, in his memory.

Harkon returned from his memories as Vicomte Vos asked the witness, "When did you next see the Archbishop?"

"The following morning, I was at my desk in the duke's office drafting a charter when the Duke and the Archbishop came into the duke's office. My desk was inconspicuously off to one side of the duke's work area so it wouldn't interfere with whatever the Duke was engaged in."

"When the Duke and Archbishop entered, did the duke ask you to leave?"

"No, he didn't. I usually remained at my desk when he had meetings, since I would be drafting any of the documents that might result from such meetings. I drafted the first draft and approved a final draft before reading the documents to Duke William for his final approval."

"Were you able to hear the conversation between the Duke and the Archbishop?"

"Yes, I was."

"And what was your understanding of this conversation between Duke William and the Archbishop?"

"I understood that the Archbishop was delivering a message from King Edward of England, that William was to be his heir and the successor king of England upon his death."

"Was there any discussion regarding the boys Archbishop Robert had brought with him?"

"Yes, the boys were surety for Earl Godwine's loyalty to Edward, including his choice of William as his heir."

"Thank you, Father John." Vos turned to the Court to add, "I have no further questions of this witness, Your Honor," and returned to counsel table.

"Earl Godwineson?" inquired the Chief Justice.

"Yes, Your Honor, I do have a few questions of this witness."

Leofwine and Harold had discussed the possible testimony of this witness over their wine after the evening meal. If he testified fully about his work for William, it would open a door of inquiry that Leofwine considered a pure gift. He hadn't been able to have any of the prior witnesses testify on a point he really wanted to nail down. Now, it looked as if this witness's testimony had just handed that point to him on a silver platter.

"Father John, you have testified that you were present when Archbishop Robert informed Duke William of King Edward's message, did you not?"

"Yes, I was there."

"And during that conversation to which you were privy, what, if anything did you see the Archbishop give to the Plaintiff?"

"Looking mystified at the question," Father John replied. "I didn't see the Archbishop give the Duke anything. They were just talking."

"After the meeting with the Archbishop, did the Plaintiff tell you of anything he had been given by the Archbishop?"

Still at a loss to understand the purpose behind Leofwine's questions, the witness answered, "Other than his blessing, and I suppose you could say the Godwine hostages, I don't know of anything else given to the Duke by the Archbishop."

"Now, Father John, would it be fair to say that charters, official documents originating from the Plaintiff, orders and the like, are generally first drafted by you in accordance with the Duke's instructions?"

"Yes. After the first draft, other scriveners might produce or help produce subsequent drafts, but I reviewed the final draft and would bring it to the Duke for his approval before it is written in the final form for the Duke's mark."

"It would be fair to say, then, that any charters of lands given into the control of a person, or the right to receive the income from a source given by the Duke, you would be aware of and would have been produced under your supervision, wouldn't it?"

"Yes, that's correct."

"Did you, or anyone under your direction, produce any written charter or grant of lands or benefices from Duke William wherein he granted any such deeds, grants or other benefices to the Defendant while he was in Normandy in 1064?"

Father John hesitated a moment, while he thought about the question. Then with an apologetic glance to the Duke, replied, "No, no such documents were signed by the Duke at that time, to my knowledge."

"To your knowledge, were any such documents ever granted to the Defendant by the Duke, at any time?"

"No, not to my knowledge."

"No further questions, Your Honor," said Leofwine, returning to counsel table, satisfied the testimony had gone in the direction he had hoped.

"Redirect, Vicomte?" asked the Court.

Vos was visibly conflicted about whether to try to limit the damage caused by Father John's testimony with re-direct or to ignore the damaging testimony as if it were of no import and hope that the justices would agree. After a moment's hesitation He replied, "No, Your Honor."

The Court told the witness he was dismissed.

Father John was still puzzled by the tension his testimony had caused. Since he had been sequestered and had not heard any of the earlier testimony, he was unaware of the importance of any testimony.

As Father John left the witness stand, the Court looked to Vicomte Vos inquiringly. "I have no further witnesses, Your Honor, the plaintiff rests its case-in-chief."

"That being the case," said Chief Justice Di Vinci, "court is adjourned until nine o'clock Monday morning. If by chance, the Court's business of this afternoon is not completed as anticipated, counsel will be notified if any delay in the resumption of this matter."

Harold, Leofwine and Harkon left the courthouse pleased with the morning's results. Harold glanced around at the blue sky, shining sun and, for once, a moderate breeze, and taking in all these aspects of a lovely day, said, "Leofwine, I don't know about you, but I am taking my horse for a gallop. There is time for a good run before dinner and any planning we need to do can be done after I get some fresh air. Five days inside that courtroom and I feel like a potted plant deprived of water."

Both brother and nephew heartily agreed with Harold, practically racing each other to reach their squires to ready the horses.

August 25th, 1066
Ghent, Flanders

Harold awoke Saturday morning to what promised to be a perfect day for hunting. The sunrise was a spectacular display of pinks and oranges against blue sky and white fluffy clouds in intriguing shapes. He groaned as he realized that the chances of talking Leofwine into even half a day off to take advantage of this superb day, were slim to none at all. *This trial is my future,* he thought, *and nothing is more important than it, but what a waste of such beautiful weather! Maybe we can break for a short while this afternoon to go for a gallop at least.* With a sigh of regret of what was not to be, he headed to the dining hall of their lodgings to break the morning fast with Leofwine and Harkon.

As he entered the hall, Leofwine took one look at him, and said, "Don't even think of asking, big brother! These two days are a gift not to be taken lightly and certainly not to be wasted in hunting. There is still a lot of work to be done reviewing the Duke's testimony to make sure that everything that can be refuted will be by our witnesses. Now, come eat so we can get to work."

Bowing to the inevitable, Harold joined them at the table. Harkon and Leofwine picked up the threads of the conversation they were having. Leofwine had been saying he was undecided about who or rather what subject should lead off their defense. It was important the justices understand that in England, the king didn't own title to every parcel of land as

William did in Normandy. So the 'gift' to William of all the lands of England wasn't his to gift in the first instance. But it was easily as important that they be apprised as soon as possible of the English procedures to approve a new king once the reigning one died. Unlike Normandy, it wasn't strictly hereditary.

Harkon was of the opinion that the customs and laws regarding the choosing of the next king would best set the stage for the rest of the defense.

Harold was brought up to date of their conversation. He thought about what they were saying and then offered, "If we called Earl Morcar of Northumbria as the first witness, can't he testify to both land ownership by the king as well as procedures of the Witen? To say nothing of the fact that he was at Edward's bedside when I was nominated and he knew where I was standing, in relation to Edward. Then most of the rest of the witnesses can testify in confirmation of what Morcar said, plus add anything else that will further prove the truth of his testimony."

"I spoke with him last night just after he arrived," said Harkon. "I'll go to his lodgings and ask him to join us as soon as he is able."

An hour or so later, Morcar arrived. He was not in a pleasant frame of mind. The trip across the channel had been a rough one and he wasn't happy to be away from his responsibilities as earl for so long. However, he was wise enough and enough of a leader to realize that the stakes were high and the consequences if William were to win, dire. Although the Godwinesons were not his favorite family, he recognized that England needed Harold at this time, that he was the Witen's choice as well as Edward's, and it was his duty that he would willingly assume to be loyal to his King.

The men spent the morning reviewing the testimony that Earl Morcar would give on Monday. A specific order of testimony was developed and Morcar's mood improved as he and Harold joined their leadership talents in the plan to save England. As time for the noon meal approached, Leofwine called a halt to their discussions. He admitted that a great deal had been accomplished by the morning session and a break would do everyone good. He even relented enough to suggest their meeting after dinner with Archbishop Ealdred would likely be short enough to allow an hour or so of hawking afterwards. Morcar, although not needed for their afternoon meeting, was invited to join them for the late afternoon excursion, an invitation he readily accepted.

As anticipated, the meeting with Archbishop Ealdred did not need a great deal of time. The strategy sessions had covered most of the proposed testimony of the Archbishop. Vicomte Vos's case-in-chief had presented the expected testimony so nothing needed to be changed regarding Archbishop Ealdred's planned testimony.

For all of which Harold was very thankful. At least some of this beautiful day could be enjoyed by spending it in one of his favorite pastimes, hawking. The countryside around Ghent was gently rolling field and woods, ideal hawking grounds. Everyone had been working under extreme tension and all were grateful for the chance to put aside the problems of the realm for a few hours. Harold, even while acknowledging that his country and likely his life depended on the outcome of this trial, knew he had to turn his mind to something else, if only for a few hours, if he was going to withstand the pressures of the next few days.

August 26th, 1066
Ghent, Flanders; Count Baldwin's

As soon as William had heard Mass with Matilda and his household, he and his secretary retired to a temporary office. While he was still very annoyed at the testimony his secretary had given at trial, he had too much work to catch up on to dwell on it. In particular, a courier from his brother Bishop Ode had arrived late last night; he had yet to hear his report regarding the progress of the fleet. Among other things, he had to be certain that the courier had not spoken to anyone at the castle about his journey or his message.

The courier was ordered to report to the Duke in his office. Although now rested and fed after his long ride from Dives, he was still apprehensive about appearing before the duke, as this was the first time that he had been a courier to the duke. He had heard the tales of the duke's awesome temper and fervently hoped that he was not about to witness it. He was particularly glad Bishop Odo, knowing William had his secretary with him, had ordered a written message sent so he merely had to deliver the scroll and await any answer.

As soon as the scroll was delivered to Duke William, the courier was dismissed and Father John apprised William of the contents. As he did so, William's mood lightened considerably. Good news was always welcome, particularly after the last week! Odo reported that the ship building was virtually complete, the volunteers were obeying orders not to ravage the countryside, and recruits continued to join the expedition. But most important of all was the news from their agents in England. Harold was having a hard time keeping his levies of land troops fed and on duty. And his fleet was also in distress. Their agents reported that it was unlikely that Harold would be able to maintain his land forces much past the first week or so of September. He would also most likely return the fleet to London if the levies disbanded to harvest crops.

William set Father John to another task while he thought about the ramifications of this news. Clearly, this was not something that he could discuss with Vicomte Vos since he remained in ignorance of the existence of the fleet project. Pacing the chamber while he considered various options, he finally left his chamber and went to find Matilda. Approaching her among her women in the solar, he suggested that she leave her stitching and come for a walk with him in the gardens.

Once they were alone, William told her about Odo's message. "If Harold has to disband the levies, there will be no one to defend the coastline, even if lookouts remain on station. But more importantly, if Harold's ships are recalled to London, they won't be in a position to notice or challenge my fleet if I have it moved further north."

"But why risk moving the ships?" Matilda asked. "So far, all has gone well and there has been no alarm that a fleet capable of invading England is being built. Won't you risk drawing attention to the possibility of an invasion by you, just when the trial is coming to a close and the Court is getting close to rendering a judgment?"

"Yes, there certainly is that risk. But on the other hand, if I do have to invade, the trip across the Channel is much shorter and less dangerous if the ships sail from St. Valery-sur-Somme."

Matilda, casually pinching several dead rose blooms from a nearby bush, thought about what William had said. "If what we hear about Norway getting ready to challenge Harold's right to be king is true, I suppose it would be wise to place whatever ships we might have in a position where they would be an effective defense of our coastline from any hostile action from a northern power. It would also be prudent to be in a position where our ships could give any aid my father might need, if his coastline were to be threatened too, don't you think?"

"I had forgotten for the moment about Harald Hardrada's claims. You are quite right, though. With a little bit of encouragement, he could easily be seen as a threat to both Normandy's ports, as well as your father's. If the danger he posed were to be broadly recognized, then, of course, placing our ships in a defensive position to meet this threat, should occasion no alarm in our neighbors, including England. Thank you, my dear. I knew a walk with you would be helpful. Now I must get back to Father John and send instructions to Odo about moving the fleet."

August 27th, 1066
Day 6 of Trial, Ghent, Flanders

Harold was up and about at first light Monday morning. Today would start the real battle for his throne as Leofwine initiated the defense to William's claims in the courtroom. Although his mind accepted the arguments to be presented to the Court as well founded and legally correct, he continued to worry about the other issues. *What about the moral issues revolving around his oath? Archbishop Ealdred had assured him his soul was not in any mortal danger because of that oath, but would this court see it that way? Would the Court only see the injured innocence facade of William? Would it respond to his attempts to portray himself in righteous indignation as the wronged party?*

As he met Leofwine and Harkon at the chapel for Mass, he thought that there had likely never been an occasion for more heartfelt prayer at Mass than this morning.

No word had come from court that there would be any delay in starting this Monday morning session on time. All the parties were in court and prepared to start when the bailiff announced the entrance of the Justices and the opening of court. Chief Justice Di Vinci reminded the parties that the Plaintiff had rested his case at the close of Friday's session and asked if the defense was ready to proceed.

"We are, Your Honor," replied Leofwine.

"You may call your first witness, then," responded Justice Di Vinci.

"The defense calls Morcar, Earl of Northumbria to the stand."

Richard Vos intended to be particularly attentive to this Earl as a witness. He had learned that in the past there had not been a cordial connection between the lords of the northern part of England and the southern parts. The earls of Northumbria had no particular liking for the Godwine family. This earl had led a revolt against the defendant's brother Tostig when he had been Earl of Northumbria. But this earl had also allowed his widowed sister to marry Harold and become his queen.

Richard had no idea how this factor would change the dynamics of the relationship and the Earl's testimony, if at all. He was hopeful that enough of the historical animosity remained that he could utilize it on cross-examination. As Earl Morcar took his place on the witness stand, Vos observed his confident demeanor and large physical size. He had the fleeting thought that they truly made these English Viking offspring in the large Scandinavian model!

"Please state your name and title, if any," asked Leofwine of the witness.

"Morcar Leofricson, Earl of Northumbria, England."

"Earl Morcar, do you hold title to lands in Northumbria?"

"Yes, I do."

"Did you receive the lands that you hold from the late King Edward of England?"

"I received some of my lands from King Edward but not all of them."

"Where is your title to the lands not received from King Edward derived from?"

"From years ago when there was a king of Northumbria, prior to the time when Northumbria agreed to join with Wessex under one High King. Much of the land in

177

Northumbria was acquired by settlement by Norsemen raiders—by conquest, if you will, not by grant of the King of Wessex. Those lands have been in my family for several generations."

"Have you pledged fealty to the King of England?"

"Yes, I have."

"What benefit, if any, did you receive in return?"

"I was made Earl of Northumbria to administer the fief for King Edward."

"Had your father been the earl before you?"

"Not directly before me. When he died, King Edward gave the administration of Northumbria to Tostig Godwineson."

"How long did Tostig remain as the earl?"

"About eleven years."

"Do you know of the circumstances wherein he ceased to be the Earl of Northumbria?"

"Yes, I do."

"Would you describe those circumstances to the Court?"

"In late 1064, there was yet another murder of a noble's son while at Earl Tostig's court. This event led to the leading nobles and thanes of Northumbria marching to King Edward to demand that Tostig be replaced."

"Are you saying that Northumbria revolted against King Edward?" asked Leofwine in apparent dismay.

"No, not at all. We, the important leaders of Northumbria were petitioning our King to enforce the laws of England and customs of Northumbria which Tostig was ignoring, contrary to his oath taken when he became earl."

"What was the outcome of the petition to King Edward?"

"King Edward listened to our petition, recognized the justice of it, and removed Tostig as Earl of Northumbria, restoring the earldom to me as my father's heir."

"And both as the Earl of Northumbria and a leading landowner in the north, were you a member of King Edward's Witenagermot?"

"Yes, I was and had been for a number of years since my father died.

"Earl Mocar, you just mentioned that Earl Tostig was 'ignoring the laws and customs of Northumbria, contrary to his oath taken when he became earl'. What were you referring to?"

"It is English law and custom that when a person accepts a fief or title, he pledges his loyalty to his people to rule justly and in accordance with law just as they pledge their loyalty to him, signifying their acceptance of his right to be their lord."

"In the event that the overlord does not honor his oath to rule justly and in accordance with law, what are the consequences, if any?"

"Then the vassals are released from their oath of loyalty to him, and can appeal to the oath-breaker's overlord for relief, which is what happened in Northumbria in '64."

While listening to this testimony by Morcar, Vicomte Vos desperately sought to find some nuggets of testimony that could be exploited on cross-examination to William's benefit. The testimony regarding the titles to lands was a blow to William's claim that King Edward had gifted all of the lands of England to William. Since not all the justices were from the continent, they would understand completely the concept of land ownership which did not derive from a grant of the sovereign. But, perhaps something could be made of the revolt against Tostig, their liege lord, duly appointed to the position by King Edward. Could the English be painted as a nation of oath-breakers? None of whom could be trusted to be honest and truthful or stand by their sworn word? Vos's attention was caught by Leofwine's next question.

"Earl Morcar, were you present in the king's chamber, at the time of King Edward's death?"

"Yes, I was."

"What, if anything, did you hear King Edward say just prior to his death?"

"I heard him say that he gave his kingdom into the care of Harold Godwineson, Earl of Wessex."

"As a leading landholder and councilor to the king, is it your understanding that under the laws and customs of England, this declaration by the dying king would make Harold Godwineson the next king?"

"No, it did not. It certainly was a strong reason for the Witenagemot to consider the person named, but the members of the witen did not have to agree with the King's choice. They could refuse to give their fealty to that person and chose another."

"Would any person the Witten might consider have to be an Aetheling, a son of royalty?"

"No, it could be anyone the council members believed capable of leading the county wisely and able to defends its borders, particularly in times when the Aetheling might be under-age and a regency dangerous for the country."

"At the death of King Edward, did the you as a member of the witen or any other member of the witen that you are aware of, give any consideration to the Aetheling Edgar from Hungary?"

"Yes, I did, as did many of the other councilors."

"What was your understanding of the witen's conclusion regarding the claims of Edgar the Aetheling?"

"The consensus was that he was too young and inexperienced to lead England in the face of all the known threats against England at this time."

"My Lord, to your knowledge, was the witen aware that Duke William of Normandy believed he had been named as the rightful heir to King Edward some years earlier and therefore became king upon Edward's death?"

"Yes, they were. The witen had been apprised of Duke William's claim by Earl Harold right at the beginning of its meeting after King Edward's death."

"What was your understanding of the response, if any, of the witen to that claim?"

"It was utterly rejected."

"Were any grounds for such a rejection discussed by the members of the witen in your presence?"

"Yes."

"What was your understanding of the grounds for such a rejection of Duke William's claim discussed by the witen?"

"The witen councilors discussed several grounds for the rejection of Duke William's claim. In the first instance, even assuming that King Edward had named Duke William his heir in 1051 or '52, such a nomination was not irrevocable by the King, nor binding on the leading earls, clergy and thanes which comprised the witen at the time of the King's death fourteen years later. A member of the witen who had agreed to such a nomination in '51 and was still a member of the witen would be the only one who might be bound to support such a nomination."

"Are you saying that none of the current councilors comprising King Edward's witan in January of this year were his councilors in 1051 or 1052 when he is said to have named Duke William as his heir?"

"It is my understanding that Duke William named the Earls of Northumbria, Mercia, and Wessex, Archbishop Robert of Jumiéges and Archbishop Stigand as the witen councilors who agreed to support his nomination. Of those men, only Archbishop Stigand was alive when the Witenage-mot met in January this year and he did not join in any of the discussions."

"When the witen met after the death of King Edward, were there any other major reasons discussed for the rejection of Duke William's claim?"

"Yes, there were several other important considerations discussed."

"What were such other considerations?"

"We discussed that even if King Edward had made such a declaration in 1051, or '52, he revoked it by his deathbed nomination of King Harold. We determined that under our law, a dying declaration would take precedence over any prior choice. And lastly, after having suffered through years of foreign kingship under Cnute and his sons, nobody wanted another foreigner, who was not even a legitimate son, as their king."

"Drawing your attention to King Edward's chamber as he lay dying, was King Harold in the room at that time?"

"Yes, he was."

"And where was he in relation to the King?"

"He was standing at the foot of the bed, next to me on my left with my brother, the Earl of Mercia on King Harold's left."

"Did you see any indication, by word or change of body, that the Defendant made any effort or attempt to influenced King Edward's words in any way?"

"No, I did not. King Harold was as surprised by King Edward's words as the rest of us. Nobody was expecting him to name Harold."

'Who was placed closest to King Edward when he spoke naming Harold of Wessex?"

"King Edward's confessor and Archbishop Ealdred were at his side helping support him in a half-reclining position as he spoke to Queen Edith and the assembled earls and prelates. His physicians were also at the head of the bed, ready to give any aid they could."

"Were the words appointing the Defendant the only words uttered or actions taken by the dying King, at this time?"

"No, when he named King Harold, he also specifically pointed at him. King Edward then went on to praise and console Queen Edith and he mentioned his faithful retainers and asked that King Harold allow them to return to Normandy if they so wished."

"To your knowledge, during the week or so that King Edward had become ill and bedridden, was he ever left alone?"

"Not to my knowledge. His doctors, confessor, Queen Edith were constantly at his side. Members of the court were in and out of the room checking on the state of his health. Much of the time, the King appeared to be asleep or unconscious. He would periodically awaken, speak with those tending him and then fall silent again, until the last time when he named Earl Harold his heir."

"Prior to becoming ill, to your knowledge, had King Edward shown any indication that he had selected an heir?"

"To my knowledge, he had not made any specific pronouncement regarding an heir."

"In the days just prior to his death, was there speculation among the councilors of Edward's witen that King Edward would name a successor?"

"Yes, there was some general talk about if he would name anyone his successor. The persons I spoke with, at least, assumed that if King Edward named anyone, it would be the Aetheling Edgar. Edgar was being raised as an Aethling, presumably as Edward's heir."

Throughout the Earl's testimony, Vicomte Vos paid close attention, seeking any potential opportunity to interrupt, disrupt and challenge the witness. However, knowing how importance the substance of the Earl's testimony was to the defense, Leofwine had been extremely careful to avoid any grounds for Vos's objections. The time when Vos must cross-examine the witness was rapidly approaching. And all the while, he was keenly aware that at his side, Duke William was getting more and more angry at how the testimony, if believed by the Justices, was eroding his position and testimony.

As Morcar answered this last question, Leofwine advised the Court that he had no further questions of this witness, and returned to defendant's table.

The Court, taking note of the time, ordered that it being nearly time for the midday break, announced the recess of the court, dismissing the witness until court reconvened at two o'clock when his cross-examination would begin.

As William and Vos left the courtroom, William grumbled to Vos, 'What was all that nonsense about land titles not coming from the king? Who else would they come from? Morcar certainly doesn't expect the Justices to believe him, does he?"

Vos shook his head uncertainly. "I'm not sure whether they will believe it or not. Certainly that is not the case here in Normandy where it is well understood that Rollo received a grant of the Normandy lands from the French king. But England has a different history of separate kingdoms dividing the island and Danish Norsemen raiding and then settling on land they essentially conquered. It wasn't given to them, they took it. And were paid tribute not to take more! Unfortunately, I think it likely to be true that the English king does not have the same power over the ownership of the land holdings of his subjects as you do."

This definitely not being the answer that William was expecting, he retreated into silence for the remainder of the ride to his father-in-law's castle.

Upon resumption of the trial, Vos immediately assumed an aggressive manner as he approached the witness Morcar to start his cross examination. In an accusatory tone of voice, he stated, rather than asked the witness, "Earl Morcar, you swore an oath of fealty to Tostig Godwineson when he became Earl of Northumbria, didn't you?"

"Yes, I did."

"And you broke that pledge of loyalty and revolted against your sworn lord, didn't you?"

"No, I didn't."

No, you didn't revolt against Earl Tostig, is that your testimony?" queried Vos in apparent disbelief.

"No, I didn't break my pledge of fealty," answered Morcar with an almost bored tone.

"So you admit you revolted against your liege lord," challenged Vos.

"No," explained Morcar as if to a dimwitted child. "As I said before, we, the leaders of Northumbria, petitioned the King to enforce the laws and customs of Northumbria, and England, as we had every right to do, since Earl Tostig was in constant breach of his oath to us to govern according to law."

"You would have this Court believe that a very large group of armed men, capable of violence against the King, or any who opposed them, demanding to speak with the King, wasn't a revolt, wasn't an armed insurrection against their sworn liege lord, is that your testimony?" asked Vos, incredulously.

"There was no violence or threat to the King. The leaders of Northumbria and the King and some of his councilors, including the defendant, met peacefully with King Edward. After hearing our petition, King Edward agreed that Tostig would be replaced."

Having made as much as he could of Northumbia's defiance of Tostig, Vos changed subjects hoping to expose another weak link in the Earl's testimony. "Earl Morcar, you testified that you were at the bedside of King Edward when he is said to have given England into the care of the Defendant. At that time, isn't it true that you knew that King Edward had already named Duke William as his heir?"

"I vaguely remember something being said to that effect by my father, years ago, but it was a long time ago."

"Are you telling this Court that the naming of an heir is not important enough to remember at the time of the king's death?" asked Vos, as if utterly amazed at Morcar's response.

"It was obviously important to my father since he is the one who is supposed to have agreed to support William as Edward's heir, but that was a long time ago and my father has been dead many years now. Any such agreement to support Duke William as Edward's choice died with my father."

"So the word of Northumbria is as easily broken as his oath of fealty to his Earl, isn't it?"

"Objection, Your Honor," thundered Leofwine, jumping to his feet. "Counsel is badgering and insulting the witness, with no relevance to the supposed question!" Leofwine hoped that his timely intervention would give the volatile Earl Morcar a chance to get control of himself before he came flying from the witness stand to attack Vos for the insult to his father and himself.

"I withdraw the question, Your Honor. Vos had sought to rile the witness, and this last 'almost' question had certainly done so. Morcar was controlling himself with obvious difficulty. "Earl Morcar, you are related to the Defendant, aren't you?"

"Yes." Morcar barely said the word, clearly not about to give his questioner anything other than the bare minimum answer.

"What is that relationship."

"He married my sister."

Vos, beginning to be annoyed at the abrupt answers, asked. "When did the Defendant marry your sister?"

"This past spring," came the brief answer.

"And was your sister as his consort the price of your vote in the witen for the defendant as King?" smoothly asked Vos.

This time, Morcar truly came near to leaving the witness stand, as he snarled his answer, "My vote in the witen wasn't for sale, and never would be and anyone who suggests otherwise is a liar!"

Vos turned to the Justices to announce he had no further questions for this witness and, returning to counsel table, sat down.

Leofwine immediately rose and advised the Court that he had no redirect questions. He had realized during the latter part of the questioning that Morcar was handling Vos's questions very well on his own and to engage in re-direct would dilute the impression that it was Morcar who was in control of the testimony, not Vos.

With court adjourned for the day, Leofwine and Harold left the courtroom with Morcar, congratulating him on his testimony, particularly in the face of Vos's insults. As Leofwine explained to Morcar, who was still ready to do bodily harm to Vos, such tactics only went to show just how much damage Morcar's testimony was causing William's case.

Slowly Morcar regained his good humor.

August 28th, 1066
Day 7 of Trial, Ghent, Flanders

Harkon was awake early in anticipation of the testimony today. He had spent the previous evening listening to Leofwine and Harold as they fine-tuned the testimony. Harkon eagerly awaited the effect it would have on the Justices and on Duke William, even though the Duke knew the essence of it. But William was undoubtedly hoping Vos would be able to exclude this damaging evidence.

Harkon had been working closely with Archbishop Ealdred during the preparation for the trial and had come to appreciate the intelligence and competence of the prelate. Harkon had often thought during their association that if ever there was a man to have in your corner in times of trouble, the Archbishop was one he would pick. His testimony held the key to refute so many aspects of the case presented by William. And his demeanor and self-assurance made it very hard to doubt whatever he said. *Now if the Justices are as impressed with the Archbishop as I am,* mused Harkon, *all will be well.*

By now, everyone was well aware of the procedures for the start of another day of trial and they were quickly and smoothly accomplished. Leofwine call Archbishop Ealdred to the stand, the oath was given and the day began.

"Please state your name and position," asked Leofwine.

"Ealdred, originally a monk at Winchester, formerly abbot of Tavistock, Devon, formerly Bishop of Worcester and now Archbishop of the diocese of York, England."

"In your various positions within the Church, have you had the opportunity and the duty to become familiar with church documents which have been issued or authorized by the various Popes?"

"Yes, I have made it part of my life's work to research early Church writings, orders and instructions to help with the organization of the church and its dealings with the people and governments. Past records aid in keeping the Church faithful to the intent and instructions of its founders while changing only what is needed to keep abreast of the current needs of its congregation."

Leofwine, handed a letter to the witness. "Your Grace, I show you this document. Are you familiar with it?"

"Yes I am."

"Can you identify this document?"

"Yes. It is a report from Bishop Ostia of the 786 Papal Legatine to England about the actions of the Bishops of the Legate and the results of their meetings in Canterbury, Mercia and Northumbria, as well as the cannons which they proposed and were adopted by the Witens of Mercia and Norumbria."

"Have you had any occasion to make reference to this letter in recent years?"

"Yes, I have."

"When did you first have occasion to make any reference to this document?"

"When King Edward summoned me to a meeting along with Earl Harold, to discuss seeking to bring Edmund the Exile from Hungary to England in early 1054. Since we were discussing the legitimate succession of persons to the throne of England, I asked King Edward if he was aware of the cannon promulgated by the Legatine of 786."

"What if anything, did you do next?"

"I told him about the report by Bishop Ostia. I arranged for the letter to be sent to me from Canterbury where it was archived so he could see a copy of it."

"And is it your sworn testimony that this document now before you is the true and accurate copy of the report of the doings of the Legatine Council of 786, sent to Pope Hadrian, and retained in the official church records at Canterbury?"

"I do."

"Your Honors, I ask that this document which has previously been marked for identification as Defendant's Exhibit A be entered into evidence in this matter."

"Objection, Your Honor. This is not the original document. It also is almost 300 years old. Many cannons, customs and laws have greatly changed in the past 300 years. I submit that it is irrelevant to any proceedings held today."

"Your Honors," responded Leofwine, "since the original report was sent to the Pope at Rome, the document kept here in England as the official church record of the proceeding, cannot be anything but a copy. As to its authenticity, I would call your attention to the fact that the seal of Bishop Ostia is visible on the document, as well as the witness signatures of several of the other attending bishops. As to its relevance, I will establish that by further testimony of this witness."

Chief Justice Di Vinci addressed the parties. "The Court was previously made aware that the admission into evidence of this document was challenged by the Plaintiff. It is the ruling of this Court that the Court will allow the admission of the document, subject to its relevance being established by further testimony. If not so established, it will be excluded. The clerk may provisionally enter Defendant's Exhibit A into evidence."

William, sitting at plaintiff's table, had a difficult time determining the appropriate culprit to glare at and display his anger and disgust at the ruling; Vos for not being more voracious in his objections or the Court for allowing the document's entry, even provisionally. Turning to Vos as he sat down, William snarled, "Get the Court to take a break now—right now, before any more damage is done! We need to talk!"

Knowing better than to argue with William in this mood, Vos came to his feet again, addressing the Court, "Your Honors, since opposing counsel still has what will likely be lengthy testimony of this witness and it is nearly time for the mid-morning break, I would move that we adjourn at this time for thirty minutes."

"I have no objection, Your Honors," added Leofwine.

Chief Justice announced, "Court is adjourned until 10:45 at which time testimony will resume."

As soon as William and Vos reached a secluded place outside the courtroom, William rounded on Vos. "You were supposed to keep that letter out of evidence! What happened? Why will Ealdred be allowed to read it?"

"William," responded Vos, "I told you I would do my best to keep it out of evidence but there was no certainty I would be successful. At least is only provisionally accepted. But unless you know something I don't know, my research has failed to come up with any document which would indicate the Cannons have ever been repealed by Church or Witen. That being so, it is more than likely the letter will be permanently admitted into evidence. There is only so much that I can do, William. Facts are facts."

As they returned to the courtroom for the resumption of Archbishop Ealdred's testimony, William was only physically present. His mind was one hundred forty miles away, figuring out sailing schedules, tides and preparedness of his fleet which should be gathered at St. Valery-sur-Somme by now or at least close to being gathered there. If this trial continued the way it appeared to be heading, William was becoming more certain the outcome would not be in his favor. In which case, he needed to be prepared to act quickly and decisively. The first thing on his agenda was to question Vos to get his estimate of how much longer the actual trial would take. Then, how long for a decision. He doubted Richard would have anything other than a 'best guess' as to how long the Justices might take before reaching a decision but that would be better than nothing. If he had a courier ready to travel as soon as the trial ended, preparations to load supplies and armaments could be completed so that by the time the Court reached a decision, barring contrary winds, it would be only a matter of days before the fleet could sail.

As William ignored the trial before him and concentrated on the implementation of his plans, Leofwine resumed his direct examination of Archbishop Ealdred.

"Your Grace, would you please read to the Court the paragraph beginning Cannon number 15 in Defendant's exhibit A?"

The witness recited from the exhibit, "'Illegitimate children are excluded from their father's inheritance and in particular, they are excluded from succession to the Kingdom.'"

"Were these Cannons adopted by the Witenagemots of Northumbria and Mercia?"

"The legate's letter to the Pope is to inform him of the actions taken by the Legatine Council and that their actions were approved by the Witens."

"Your Grace, to your knowledge has there been any illegitimate person as king in England since this Cannon was adopted?"

"No, there has not been."

"In your capacity as the leading prelate of England, have you any knowledge that Cannon number 15 has ever been revoke or amended?"

"In my examination of church records and as an archbishop of the Church in England, I have found no evidence that this Cannon number 15 has ever been revoked or amended. It is still in effect today."

From his seat at the back of the courtroom, Harkon smiled in delight at the expressions of the justices upon hearing this testimony. They had known the letter was challenged as admissible into evidence but not the content of the letter. There was considerable impact upon them at hearing of the prohibition against illegitimacy. Even more so at the actual testimony of the archbishop that the Cannon had been followed to this day and was still effective law. Their expressions told Harkon that they considered this an important piece of evidence in the case.

Although Leofwine had further questions to put to the Archbishop, Harkon silently applauded his tactic of taking a moment to go to his papers at his desk, as if looking for a particular document, before making his motion and resuming his examination. He was innocently avoiding any chance of diluting the impact of Ealdred's testimony upon the justices by rushing into the next topic of inquiry. So far, today's testimony was going exactly as planned.

Addressing the Court with the 'found' notes in hand, Leofwine moved that the letter be accepted as relevant and permanently admitted into evidence. As anticipated, Vicomte Vos renewed his objection to its admittance, arguing that merely because there had been no illegitimate person as king, did not establish that such a selection was brought about in observance of Cannon number 15. Leofwine countered with his argument that unless the Plaintiff could offer evidence to establish that the Cannon had been repealed or revoked or amended, it remained in effect as a matter of law.

Chief Justice Di Vinci, glancing at each of the Justices, took a quick poll and announced the Court's decision that the letter was relevant and would be admitted into evidence without proviso.

Leofwine, graciously refraining from looking smug, while a very glum Vos returned to his counsel table, resumed his inquiry of Archbishop Ealdred. "Your Grace, you have spoken of conversations in 1054 with King Edward regarding the Aetheling, Edward the Exile. What, if anything, resulted from those conversations?"

"King Edward sent me on a mission to Germany to obtain help in gaining permission to visit Edward the Exile in Hungary to persuade him to come to England and assume his birthright as an Aetheling and Edward's likely heir."

"Did you visit Edward the Exile?"

"No, I was unable to do so, but I did ascertain that he was alive and well and had received the request to return to England. It was not until a few years later in 1057, that he was persuaded to come to England with his family."

"When Edward the Exile returned to England, did he assume the duties and rights of an Aetheling?"

"No, he died shortly after entering England."

"What happened, if anything to his family?"

"His children, including his son, Edgar, who was only about four years old, were taken into care by Queen Edith and raised in the royal household."

"Your Grace, were you present in King Edward's bed-chamber as he lay dying?"

"Yes, I was."

"Did you hear the King make any appointment of a successor?"

"Yes, I did."

"What, if anything ,did you understand the King to say?"

"Objection, Your Honor, hearsay," interrupted Vicomte Vos.

"Your Honor, in the first instance anything the king said would be a dying declaration and therefore admissible and secondly, the question asks for the witness's understanding of what was said, not the truth of the statement," quickly replied Leofwine.

"Overruled," responded the Court. "You may answer, Your Grace."

"King Edward clearly said that he gave the kingdom into the care of Harold Godwineson."

"Was the defendant in the chamber at the time that King Edward said this?"

"Yes, he was."

"Was he in a position to influence the words of the king?"

"No, he was standing some distance away, at the foot of the bed, along with some other earls, when the King pointed to him and spoke."

"Were you a member of the Witenagemot that considered who should be the successor to King Edward, once he had died?"

"Yes, I was."

"Was the Witenagemot required to accept the choice of successor as named by King Edward?"

"No, the earls, prelates and thegns could choose not to accept as their king the choice of the prior king. It was an individual choice whether each man's loyalty and pledge of fealty was given or not."

"Did the Witenagemot accept the man named by King Edward, Harold Godwineson?"

"Yes, they did. It was unanimous."

"Did you participate in the coronation of Harold of Wessex?"

"Yes, I did.

"Would you describe to this court, the procedures of the crowning of the king in England?"

"This coronation took place in King Edward's newly consecrated Westminster Abbey. In accordance with custom, I laced the crown upon the head of Harold. The leaders of England then gave their oath to the new King that they accepted him as their king and the King gave his oath to the subjects present that he would rule justly and in accordance with custom and law. Them, as Archbishop of York, the highest ranking prelate in England, I anointed him with Holy Oil and consecrated him as King of England. Throughout the ceremony I was assisted by Stigand, Bishop of Winchester and other high ranking churchmen."

"Just one further question, Your Grace. If a person is forced against his will and out of legitimate concern for the safety or lives of others dependent upon him, to swear an oath before God, is that oath binding upon him?"

"Objection, Your Honor. That calls for speculation from the witness. Neither has the witness been qualified as an expert to render such an opinion, for which no foundation has been laid," interjected Vos.

"Your Honor, surely it is not speculation for an archbishop of the Church to give an opinion on the sanctity of an oath given before God. Further there has been no objection to, or claim that, the witness is anything other than an archbishop of the Church, duly appointed to the See of York. If an archbishop of the Church cannot determine if such an oath is binding, then who can?"

"The witness may answer," ruled the Court.

With an air of ecclesiastical certainty, Archbishop Ealdred answered, "In order for an oath before God to be binding it must be honestly made and with a free will. An oath taken in order to prevent reasonably anticipated harm to himself or another is not made of the oath-taker's free will and is not binding in the sight of man or God. The sin falls on the one forcing such an oath to be taken."

"Thank you, Your Grace." Addressing the Court, Leofwine added, I have no further questions of this witness, Your Honor."

"In that case," replied the Chief Justice, "we will take the noon break at this time. Vicomte, you may begin your cross-examination of the witness when Court reconvenes at two o'clock this afternoon."

"Did you see their faces when they realized what Bishop Ostia's letter said?" asked Harkon jubilantly as the defense team left the courthouse. "It was priceless! It was almost as if they were asking, 'then what are we here for?' And William sure wasn't pleased with Vos. I wonder how long he will remain a vicomte. The Duke doesn't take kindly to those who are supposed to be protecting his interests, when they fail."

Leofwiwne and Harold, knowing there was still a long road ahead of them before they could claim victory enjoyed Harkon's high spirits and were encouraged by it but remained cautious about rejoicing too soon.

Putting aside his anger at Vos, William used the time after court ended to elicit the information he needed to implement his plans for the fleet. With these thoughts in mind, and using the pretext that he was anxious about being away from the affairs of the duchy for so long, he asked Vos how much longer he thought the actual trial would take.

A bit surprised that William was conversing pleasantly with him, Vos thought a moment before answering. "According to their witness list, Leofwine intends to call three more witnesses, and probably Harold, after them. So say two days for the witnesses, two to three more days for Harold and cross-examination, five more days will probably be pretty close for the end of actual testimony. Add another day for closing statements of counsel and then it goes to the justices for deciding. How long they will take to come to a decision is anyone's guess. There is a lot of testimony to review and consider in arriving at a decision."

William absorbed this information, translating it into courier travel time and loading ships. He came to the conclusion that if he dispatched a courier to his brother Bishop Odo to ready the fleet for sailing on short notice, it could be ready to sail as soon as there was a Court ruling. He would have enough time, if he left for St. Valéry at the close of the trial, to be with the fleet and ready to sail as soon as a fast courier brought the Court ruling, if it was against him.

In the meantime, Vos would play his part here in Ghent. He would do what he could to convince the justices of the legitimacy and rightness of his cause, with no need to know about any contingency plan.

Returning to court after the noon break, Vos was not looking forward to his cross-examination of Archbishop Ealdred. He had been a formidable witness for the defense and it would be difficult to impugn his testimony. Nonetheless, he started out trying to establish that surely the Archbishop had not been with King Edward every minute so that it was possible the Defendant had opportunities to influence or force the dying King to name him his successor. That avenue of attack was counterproductive since it merely established that once the king had taken ill, Harold was busy with affairs of the kingdom and King Edward was either unconscious or surrounded by his doctors and confessor. Prior to his sudden illness, Edward had been hale and hardy, able to enjoy a day's hunting and fully capable of resisting any efforts to force him to name a successor other than the presumptive heir, Aetheling Edgar.

Since Vos could offer no evidence that the Cannons adopted in 786 had ever been overturned, there was little he could do to dilute the impact of that testimony, try as he might. For the afternoon session, he hammered at the archbishop but with little effect. He gratefully recognized the fading afternoon light and announced an end to his cross-examination. Leofwine had no re-direct of the archbishop. Chief Justice Di Vinci adjourned court for the day.

August 29th, 1066
Day 8 of Trial, Ghent Flanders

The defense team had discussed at length the previous evening which witness would have the most impact to solidify the archbishop's testimony, particularly with respect to the succession. It was decided that Leofwine would call Queen Edith as his first witness of the day.

In the pre-trial meetings, Edith had made it clear that she was not particularly enthusiastic about being called as a witness. However, faced with the possibility of William winning his case unless the strongest defense was mounted, she had agreed to do what she could to defeat William's claims.

Leofwine started his examination establishing the basic background information: the witness was Edith Godwinedottir, dowager Queen of England, widow of King Edward of England and sister to the defendant, King Harold II. She had married King Edward when she was twenty-five years old and Edward was forty-three and had been married for twenty-one years. Asked if her years of marriage were happy years, Edith answered: "Like most married people, we had our ups and downs, but except for the time in1051 when he was wrongly persuaded to send me to a nunnery—"

"Objection, Your Honor," Vos interrupted. "There is no foundation for the characterization that Edward 'was wrongly persuaded' to send Queen Edith anywhere at that time."

"Sustained, the characterization is stricken," ruled the Court.

"My Lady," asked Leofwine, continuing with what he considered to be the important part of her testimony, "what action, if any, did King Edward take in regard to you in 1051?"

"My husband ordered me to retire to the nunnery at Winchester."

"At that time, did you believe that you were permanently banished from Edward's presence and as his queen?"

"No. I believed Edward was just angry with my father and would soon get over it, which he did. I returned to the royal household at King Edward's side and bed."

"After you and King Edward were reconciled, did King Edward ever tell you that he had named Duke William as his heir?"

"No, he never said anything to suggest that. If he had done that, he would never have sent Archbishop Ealdred to find Edward the Exile and his family to return them to England."

"What position, if any, did young Edgar hold in the royal household after his father died?"

"Well, technically, he wasn't an Aetheling since his father had never been a king. But King Edward, in effect, adopted him when he ruled that Edgar was to be considered an Aetheling, since he was of Saxon royal blood. So he was raised as an Aetheling within the royal household."

"How would you describe Edward's spirituality during the years of your marriage?"

"Throughout our marriage Edward was very generous to the church and to the abbeys and convents. As the years went by and it became less and less likely that a child would be born to us, Edward became more engaged in a spiritual and holy lifestyle. By about 1045 or so, he started the building of Westminster Abby, near to the castle. It became his obsession to complete the abbey, have it consecrated and become the place for his grave. As the Abbey became a reality its construction occupied a great deal of Edward's time and attention, Edward turned increasingly to Harold to manage and direct the political and everyday affairs of the country."

"How would you describe King Edward's health during the months prior to his becoming ill in December 1065?"

"Well, he was getting older, of course, but he still was an avid hunter and very much enjoyed the chase. Sometimes if it was a choice of using his energy to attend to state matters, or to go hunting, he would have my brother Harold take care of the matters of state so he could join the hunt."

"Drawing your attention to the period of time just before the last several weeks of Edward's life, had King Edward been ill or sickly?"

"No, he seemed his normal self. He was looking forward to the consecration of the Abbey which was to take place in a few weeks."

"When he became ill, were you expecting his illness to be serious?"

"Not at first. After all he was 64 years old, so any illness had to be viewed as possibly serious. But initially, it didn't seem that this illness was anything special. It was only as the week progressed and he became increasingly debilitated that everyone realized just how serious an illness it was."

"In your opinion, and given your intimate knowledge of your husband, do you believe King Edward knew he was dying, that he only had a short time to live?"

"The last several days before he died, yes. He would lose consciousness for several periods of time just prior to his death. I believe he understood exactly what was happening when he regained consciousness for the final time. He was very lucid when he spoke his last words."

"Were you at his bedside at the time of his death?"

"Yes, I was."

"Where was King Harold at the time of King Edward's final words?"

"My brother was in the king's chamber, standing at the end of King Edward's bed."

"From where you were situated, did you observe any effort or attempt by Harold to influence the actions of King Edward?"

"No, he couldn't have. He wasn't close enough to Edward physically to do so and there were too many other people surrounding Edward to permit anyone to use any force to make Edward say anything he didn't want or intend to say."

"What was your understanding of the meaning of King Edward's last words?"

"His meaning was very clear. He appointed my brother Harold as his choice to be his heir and the next king of England."

"As the wife of King Edward for 21 years, do you believe Edward would have endangered his immortal soul by breaking a binding prior promise that named William his heir?"

"No, Edward would never have done such a thing. Knowing he was dying, he would never have endangered his mortal soul by nominating Harold if he had made such a promise."

"No further questions, Your Honor. Your witness, counsel.

Vos approached Queen Edith, showing every sign of respect for her station, but remaining intent on discrediting her testimony, if he could. The most obvious place to start was her bias as the defendant's sister. "My lady, correct me if I'm wrong, but Earl Harold is your brother, is he not?"

"Objection, Your Honors," interjected Leofwine, if only to disrupt the pace Vos had hoped to get started with the witness. "Counsel must designate to whom he is referring in order for the witness to be able to truthfully respond. The

Defendant, if that is to whom counsel is referring, is not 'Earl Harold' but is King Harold II. If that is to whom counsel is referring, then he needs to properly so identify."

"I'll rephrase, Your Honors," offered Vos in an effort to get his momentum going forward again. "My Lady, the Defendant herein is your brother, is he not?

"Yes, he is."

"And throughout your marriage to King Edward, you have used your influence to advance the career of your brother, haven't you?"

"No, not particularly. Harold gained advancement because of his usefulness to Edward, and because he was one of the largest landholders in England."

"Isn't it also true that for many of the last years of your marriage, you no longer shared a bed with King Edward?"

"Yes, that is true."

"Approximately when did you stop having marital relationship with King Edward?"

"Around the time Edward was building Westminster Abbey, around 1053. As he became more engrossed with building the abbey and the status of his soul, he also became convinced that it was not only impossible to have a child but it was not God's wish that we have children. So he had Archbishop Ealdred start looking for the last Saxon royal descendant, Edward the Exile, to bring him to England."

"But Edward the so-call Exile never became heir to King Edward, did he?"

"No, he did not, but—"

"You have answered the question, My Lady. There is no question now before you."

Having done what he could to weaken Queen Edith's testimony, little as it was, Vos advised the court he had no further questions and released the witness.

Leofwine quickly determined that Vos had not done any real damage to Edith's testimony and declined re-direct examination. Edith was excused.

Archdeacon Gilbert had spent the first part of the morning sitting alone in one of the many rooms of the court's palace in accordance with the Court's order that witnesses be sequestered. He tried to concentrate on saying his beads, but the thoughts of his upcoming testimony kept intruding. What were they going to ask? Vicomte de Conches had told him what he thought the Defendant's counsel would ask, but what if he asked something different? What if something he said really hurt Duke William's case? The duke would be furious and that was not a prospect to look forward to! How he wished he had never been ordered to Rome!

A knock on the door announced one of the court's bailiffs, who entered, saying, "Archdeacon, you have been called to the courtroom."

Still saying his beads, he slowly rose to his feet and followed the bailiff to the courtroom. He was directed to the witness stand and the justices' clerk administered the oath that he would testify truthfully. He didn't dare look at the duke. He knew that if he did and met that stern visage, which clearly was telling him to remember his meetings with the Vicomte, he would be undone.

The Earl Leofwine of Essex approached and asked pleasantly, "Would you please state your name, occupation and title?"

"Father Gilbert, I am the archdeacon at the cathedral at Lisieux, Normandy."

"Now, Father Gilbert, would you please tell the court how you came to be a witness at this trial?"

"I received a court subpoena from the Defendant. It ordered me to appear here as a witness."

"Father Gilbert, did you head a delegation to Pope Alexander II in the spring of 1066?"

"Yes, I did."

"On whose behalf was this delegation sent?"

"Duke William of Normandy."

"Would you please tell the Court what were your instructions regarding the purpose of this delegation?"

"We were to inform the Pope of the of the illegal actions of Earl Harold by becoming the king of England when Duke William had been named the heir of King Edward. We were to seek the Pope's support in condemning such action, as well as obtain any help he could give to assist Duke William to his rightful throne."

"Your Honors, I move to have this witness declared a hostile witness, on the grounds that he is biased, clearly associated with the Plaintiff and partisan to his claims to the throne of England."

"Objection, Your Honors," stated Richard Vos. "This witness has been called by the Defense as its own witness. The defense knew of the association and any alleged bias before they subpoenaed his appearance."

"Counsel will approach the bench." A vigorous discussion ensued before the justices with regard to the characterization of this witness. After several minutes, the Court declared, "The Court grants the motion and declared the witness a hostile witness."

Leofwine continued with his examination, establishing that the arguments presented to the Pope to seek his support for Duke William's claims had been prepared primarily by Abbot Lanfranc of St Stephen's Abbey and Duke William.

Father Gilbert repeated to the Court the major arguments that were presented to the Pope to gain his support; that King Edward had declared William to be his heir; the designation was irrevocable; King Harold had sworn on holy relics to support Duke William's designation as heir; King Harold had usurped the throne by force and guile; Harold was forsworn and was morally corrupt, living openly with a woman without benefit of a church sanctioned marriage; and finally, that King Harold supported the illegal appointment of Archbishop Stigand to the See of Canterbury, to the detriment of the Church.

Further questions led to Father Gilbert describing meeting with some of the leading cardinals of the curia and also with the Pope, Leofwine then asked the witness, "Isn't it true that the delegation asked these cardinals to persuade the Pope to excommunicate King Harold for his perjury?"

"Yes."

"And isn't it also true the cardinals would not advise the Pope to do that?"

Father Gilbert was most uncomfortable with this question, carefully avoiding looking at Duke William as he murmured a hesitant, "Yes."

"Isn't it also true the cardinals told you that even if King Harold refused to fulfill his oath of fealty to Duke William, that was not sufficient grounds to excommunicate an anointed king?"

"Yes."

"The delegation also asked if the Pope would give Duke William a Papal banner to be displayed by Duke William as a sign of the Pope's support of Duke William's claims, didn't it?"

"Yes."

"And were you given such a banner from the Pope?"

"No."

"You were given a reason for the refusal to allow a banner to be displayed, were you not?"

As this question was asked, Father Gilbert shifted in the witness stand, obviously wishing he could avoid a response.

Finally, he said, "Yes, we were told it wouldn't be appropriate."

"Father Gilbert, in fact, were you not specifically told that such banners are only given in support of actions against the Infidels, not against fellow Christians?" barked Leofwine.

"Yes, we were," answered Gilbert softly, looking anywhere except at the duke.

"So, the Pope refused to give open support to Duke William's claims, isn't that so?"

"Well, not entirely, the cardinals—"

"Father Gilbert, just answer the question, it requires only a yes or no answer. Did the Pope openly support Duke William's claims or not—yes or no?"

"No, he did not."

"In other words, according to your testimony, if the object of the mission to Rome was to gain the open and public support of the Pope for the Plaintiff's claims, your mission failed, isn't that true?"

"Yes."

"I have no further questions of this witness, Your Honors."

Vos rose quickly from counsel table, asking his first question as he approached the witness stand. "Father Gilbert, you testified as to one purpose of the delegation to Rome. Was that the only purpose of the delegation?"

Father Gilbert visibly relaxed at the chance to answer a question to which he knew the answer, "No, it wasn't."

"What were other purposes of the delegation, if any?"

"We were also to inform the Pope that Duke William stood ready and able to help the Church in any way possible to reform the English Church and cleanse it of its problems of pluralism, hand-fast marriages, simony and worldly prelates, such as Archbishop Stigand."

"What was the response to that offer?"

"The cardinals were very appreciative and asked the delegation to convey their thanks to Duke William."

Vos went on to give Father Gilbert the chance to show the Pope's support of William's delegation, asking, "Did the Pope or the cardinals express to you any condemnation of Duke William for his claims to the English throne?"

"No, they did not," responded Gilbert emphatically.

Hoping to drive home the point a bit more, Vos asked, "Did the Pope or the cardinals give any instructions to you or the delegation that Duke William must abandon his claim to the English throne?"

Again, Father Gilbert answered in a positive tone of voice, "No, neither the Pope nor the cardinals said anything against Duke William's claim, or that he must abandon it."

Satisfied he had done what he could to negate Gilbert's direct testimony, Vos said, "I have no further questions, Your Honors."

Leofwine quickly responded, "I have just a few questions, Your Honors regarding testimony opened up on cross-examination, if I may."

"You may inquire," ordered the Court.

"Father Gilbert, you testified to the Plaintiff's offer to help reform the English Church as one of the purposes of the delegation, did you not?"

"Yes."

"Isn't it true that many of the excesses of which Archbishop Stigand could be charged, could also be applied to the Plaintiff's half-brother, Bishop Odo of Bayeux?"

"I don't know. I'm not in a position to say."

"Father Gilbert, as a Norman Archdeacon wouldn't it be fair to say that you would be more familiar with the state of the Church in Normandy than that of the Church in England?"

"I suppose so," offered Gilbert looking at a baliff standing at the door rather than Leofwine.

"And you just testified that as head of the delegation, you, on behalf of Duke William, were in a position to condemn one or more of the prelates of the English Church, as an example of the need to reform the English Church, didn't you?"

"I suppose I did," answered Gilbert checking his cassock for lint.

"But now you suddenly are 'not in a position' to say the same thing about prelates if they happen to be in Normans," challenged Leofwine. "Is that your testimony?" Without waiting for an answer from the witness, Leofwine, marched to the Defendant's table, advising the Court, as he moved, "I have no further questions, Your Honors."

Releasing the witness from further testimony, the Court adjourned for the noon break, to resume for the afternoon session at two o'clock.

The question at the noon meal was whether to put King Harold on as the next witness and then finish the defendant's case with the Bishop of Chartres testimony regarding the obligations of an oath. If it could be timed correctly, it would leave Harold's cross-examination unable to be started until the following morning, giving the Justices a chance to think about the testimony overnight. The brothers tossed the pros and cons back and forth during the meal, coming finally to the conclusion that the risk of the timing being too tight outweighed any possible advantages. So they would call the Bishop of Chartres. The assumption was that there had been enough previous testimony about the fealty oath that it wasn't necessary for Harold's testimony to precede the letter defining the obligations. There also was the fact that there would be some delay built into the afternoon's testimony, as a result of the objections to the entry of the letter into evidence expected to be argued by Vos.

After calling the Bishop of Chartres to the stand, Leofwine set about laying the foundation for his testimony: that he was Robert de Tours, Bishop of Chartres; that he had been bishop there for a year and more importantly he had previously been at Chartres when Bishop Fulbert was the bishop; as a clerk at the diocese often assisting the bishop with his correspondence.

Leofwine then showed a document to the witness asking, "Are you familiar with this document?" Upon the bishop acknowledging he was familiar with it, Leofwine asked the witness to please tell the Court how he happened to be familiar with this particular document.

"I helped Bishop Fulbert do the research needed to respond to a request from William V, Count of Poitou and Duke of Aquitaine and made a copy of his response for the diocese files. This document is the copy of his letter the bishop sent to the Duke of Aquitaine and that I made to place in the files."

"When was this letter sent to the Duke?"

"In 1020, a few years before Bishop Fulbert left the diocese."

"Is it your testimony that you wrote this document?"

"Yes, that is my writing, but I did not author it—I only copied what Bishop Fulbert wrote."

"Is it your testimony that this is a true and accurate copy of the letter sent to William V, produced for the diocese files?"

"Yes, it is."

"Your Honors, I ask that this document, marked as Defendant's Exhibit B, be entered into evidence."

"Objection, Your Honors. May we approach?"

Counsel for the parties approached the justices to argue the admissibility of Bishop Fulbert's letter.

Harold sat at Defendant's table tense and practically holding his breath, knowing how important it was to get Fulbert's letter into evidence.

Leofwine and William's counsel had already alerted the Court of the dispute to the admissibility of this document when they presented their lists of exhibits to be pre-marked before the trial. The Court had said at that time that it would rule on its admissibility at trial, after a proper foundation had been presented. Now the moment had come. Harold gave himself a mental scold and straightened his posture. He tried to look more confident than he actually felt. The muted voices of counsel as they argued their points at the side bar seemed to go on forever.

Finally, counsel returned to their tables and the Court announced its ruling: the copy of the letter was admissible and relevant to the issue of the oath of fealty.

It took all of Harold's self-control to keep from collapsing on the counsel table in relief. He didn't dare glance at plaintiff's table and William.

Harold would have been surprised had he looked at William. William did not appear upset at the ruling. In fact, he wasn't. Earlier, when Leofwine submitted his list of trial exhibits to Vos, William had been there to go over the list.

"I'm going to object to the copy of Fulbert's letter. William," Vos had said.

"Why, what does it matter?" William had replied. "It just says what the oath of fealty is about, which we all know, anyway."

"That's just it, if we all know anyway and you testify as to what the oath Harold took contained, then why do they want the letter in evidence? They have something in mind that I haven't figured out yet. I don't like it." He sighed. "It's a copy, it's not the original, so there are grounds for objecting to it."

"Whatever you say. What matters is he swore an oath on holy relics to support me and he didn't. He is foresworn in the eyes of God and is not worthy to be king. A copy of an old letter isn't going to change that."

Leofwine resumed his examination. The witness explained that Bishop Fulbert was answering an inquiry from William, Duke of Aquitaine regarding the obligations imposed by an oath of fealty. Leofwine asked the witness to read the marked paragraph from the now admitted letter.

The bishop read the letter's list of the oath-taker's obligations: "He who swears fealty to his lord ought always to have these six things in memory; what is harmless, safe, honorable, useful, easy, practicable. Harmless, that is to say that he should not be injurious to his lord in his body; safe, that he should not be injurious to him in his secrets or in the defenses through which he is able to be secure; honorable, that he should not be injurious to him in his justice or in other matters that pertain to his honor; useful, that he should not be injurious to him in his possessions; easy or practicable, that that good which his lord is able to do easily, he make not difficult, nor that which is practicable he make impossible to him."

Leofwine asked the witness to read also, another marked paragraph of the letter.

Bishop Robert, in a prelate's sermon voice, read: "However, that the faithful vassal should avoid these injuries is proper, but not for this does he deserve his holding; for it is not sufficient to abstain from evil, unless what is good is done also. It remains, therefore, that in the same six things mentioned above he should faithfully counsel and aid his lord, if he wishes to be looked upon as worthy of his benefice and to be safe concerning the fealty which he has sworn."

"Did you have any conversation with Bishop Fulbert about the meaning of the responsibilities mentioned in his letter?"

"Yes, we discussed the meaning of his words more fully while I was making the copy."

"Would it be your understanding of the Bishop's letter that the oath-taker also receives some immediate benefice, land holdings, or other advancement or advantage from 'his lord' which is what obligates him to fulfill the stated promises of the oath?"

"Yes, it would be."

"Was it your understanding from your conversations with Bishop Fulbert that there was reciprocity between the lord and the oath-taker in the swearing of an oath of fealty?" asked Leofwine.

"Yes, that is what he was saying."

"I have no further questions of this witness, Your Honor. Your witness, counsel," stated Leofwine to the Court and Vicomte Vos.

"Father Robert, isn't it true that the letter of Bishop Fulbert, which you have just read portions of, referred to an oath of fealty taken by a vassal to his lord?"

"Yes, that is true."

"But it is also true, is it not, that at the time that the Defendant swore his Oath of fealty to the Plaintiff, he was not a vassal of Duke William, that they were in fact equals?"

"I believe so, yes."

"And you are aware, aren't you, that the Defendant swore his oath to be faithful to Duke William on a Holy Bible and on holy relics?"

"Yes I am."

"No further questions, Your Honor," announced Vos casually, dismissing the witness and his testimony as not worthy of any further effort or discussion.

214

Leofwine approached the witness. "If I may inquire further, Your Honor?"

"Proceed," granted Chief Justice DiVinci.

"Father Robert, counsel questioned the applicability of Bishop Fulbert's letter when the oath of fealty was between equals rather than lord and vassal. But let me ask you, even as between equals, would there still have to be reciprocity of obligations of the parties to the oath?"

"Yes, there would," answered Bishop Robert.

"No further questions, Your Honor."

Chief Justice Di Vinci looked askance of Vicomte Vos, who stated he had no further questions, whereupon the Court dismissed the witness. The Court added that court was adjourned until nine o'clock the following morning.

Although Leofwine and Harkon tried their best to create a stress-free evening with Harold, keeping any discussions of the next day's testimony to a minimum, they were not very successful. Too much was at stake for Harold to relax, even a little bit. Harkon and Leofwine could understand. It wasn't only Harold's personal mortal future which was at stake but his spiritual status as well. And, more importantly, the future of England. What would become of the English people under a foreign, bastard king? It would be an outcome that Harold was sure he did not want to live to see. If the Court didn't agree with Archbishop Ealdred and Bishop Fulbert, if it decided he was foresworn, a pilgrimage to Jerusalem to atone for his sin might save his immortal soul, but what about England? Who would save her under William? Try as he might, there was little sleep for Harold that August night.

August 30th, 1066
Day 9 of Trial, Ghent, Flanders

As if to confirm the importance of the day, there was a beautiful sunrise that spoke of a perfect weather day to follow. Everyone was tense with the recognition of the importance of today's testimony but the parties were also relieved this trial was almost over. William especially, was in a reasonable frame of mind. He had received word from his brothers that his orders to prepare to set sail had been received and all preparations were progressing on schedule. Even the court schedule was moving in accordance with Vos' estimated timetable. Should the Court not find in his favor, all was in readiness for him to put his alternate plans into action!

Leofwine began the day by calling his final witness, King Harold II, to the witness stand. He asked the usual questions to establish Harold's, name, position, prior titles, family connections, and other pertinent background information. Leofwine then posed his questions in earnest, starting with Harold's trip to Normandy. He established that Harold had sought the permission of King Edward to leave England. While such permission was granted, Edward had thought it a foolish undertaking, and unlikely to accomplish anything and, given his knowledge of Duke William, might even cause political consequences. Edward understood Harold's desire to seek the release of his brother and nephew from continuing to be held hostage by Duke William long after Harold's father's death, but was not optimistic about a favorable outcome. He did agree, however, that first approaching Count Baldwin of Flanders, William's father-in-law, would be a wise thing to do before actually traveling to Normandy.

Continuing the direct testimony of Harold, Leofwine inquired a little more deeply into the boys held as hostage. "At that time, in 1064, were you aware of the circumstances under which the Godwine son and nephew had been given as hostages?"

"Yes, in general, but not in complete detail."

"What was your understanding of those circumstances under which your brother and nephew became hostages?"

"When my father was forgiven by King Edward, and his lands and titles were returned to him in 1052, my brother and nephew were given into the custody of King Edward as surety for my father's loyalty. However, when archbishop Robert of Jumièges fled England upon my family's return, he took the boys with him and turned them over to Duke William. King Edward did not demand their return even after my father's death in 1053 so they have remained captive in Normandy ever since."

Harold went on to testify that upon his return from Normandy, he had reported the event of the Normandy stay to King Edward, particularly that Wulfnoth had not returned to England with Harkon and Harold's men. Leofwine continued his questioning by asking, "Was King Edward curious why your brother, Wulfnoth, had not returned with you and Harkon from Normandy?"

"Yes, he was."

"What did you tell him, if anything?"

"I told him the truth. That I had not been allowed to see my brother except for a brief visit shortly before being allowed to return to England, that Wulfnoth would not be released by Duke William despite my entreaties to allow Wulfnoth to return with us. I also told him that I understood from my brief conversation with Wulfnoth, that unless I did whatever William demanded of me, he was a dead man."

Solemnly and very distinctly, Leofwine asked his next question. "At any time since your father's death, did you, as head of the Godwine family, or personally, agree to give Wulfnoth as a hostage for surety of any pledge or promise to Duke William?"

Answering emphatically and without equivocation, Harold said, "Most certainly not!. The oath of fealty was sufficient unto itself. There was no need of any hostage for I didn't pledge anything in particular to Duke William. And I certainly never agreed to leave Wulfnoth in Normandy. I had come to Normandy to get him released and returned to England!"

"Where is Wulfnoth now?"

"He remains a hostage/prisoner in Duke William's custody. William categorically refused to allow him to return with me. Short of starting a war I was unprepared for, there was nothing I could do to force him to release Wulfnoth."

At this point, the Chief Justice interrupted by suggesting to Leofwine, that since he likely had considerable more examination of the witness, this might be a good place to take the mid-morning recess. Leofwine was more than pleased with the suggestion. The justices would have time during the break to think about the justice or lack thereof in the previous testimony. Vicomte Vos was not pleased to end the testimony on that note, but there was little he could do about it. The testimony certainly did not reflect well on Duke William, but he would have to wait until he cross-examined Harold to try to change its impact. The court adjourned for thirty minutes.

When court resumed, Leofwine opened a new subject of inquiry. It would not be a lengthy inquiry but definitely one that was important. "As England's king, the primary guardian of the laws of England, would it be in accordance with English laws for a person acknowledged to be foresworn of his holy oath, to be a witness to legal documents?"

"No, it would not be in accordance with law or custom. A witness swears that his witnessing is true. If the witness is known to have lied, then obviously, his testimony as a witness cannot be trusted to be true and he cannot be a witness to any legal document or at any legal proceeding."

"In your report to King Edward, did you tell him in detail about your oath of fealty to Duke William?

"Yes, I did."

"During the period of time between your return from Normandy and King Edward's death, were you a witness under oath to any of King Edward's charters or other legal documents?"

"Yes, I was."

"Now, directing your attention to Christmastime 1065, when King Edward was taken ill—at that time, were you aware of discussions among the nobles and prelates regarding who might be the successor to King Edward should he die?"

"Yes, of course I was. It was of great concern to all of the Witenagemot since Edward had no children."

"At that same time, Christmas 1065, approximately how many persons, if any, knew of your oath to Duke William?"

Now that the questioning was approaching the subject of his oath, which had been the cause of so much soul-searching and doubt to Harold, his answer became less self-assured. Although he felt that he had resolved the moral issues and was now certain of his course of action, he was not yet completely free of the pain and guilt that the oath had cost him. Answering hesitantly, he said, "I'm not sure of an actual number. Certainly all of my men who were with me in Normandy. I had told King Edward of it (I don't know if he told Queen Edith), my sister. Edith, the mother of my children, knew of it. Several other nobles of the witen and my confessor also knew of it."

"Did any of these persons, who knew of your oath to support William suggest to you at this time, Christmas 1065, when King Edward was ill, that since you had taken an oath of fealty to Duke William, you could not be considered to succeed King Edward, even though you had been *sub-regulus* to King Edward for several years?"

"No, no one said any such thing."

"What were the topics of discussion among the Witen, that you know of, regarding the person most likely to be Edward's successor?"

"Mostly the discussion was whether the Atheling—Edgar, as a blood heir of the Saxon royal line of kings, was a viable choice to succeed Edward. The concern was that he was only a boy without any training, who had not been raised in England and spoke hesitant English."

"Was there any discussion of which you were aware, that William, Duke of Normandy might be Edward's successor?"

"No, there was no suggestion of William as a possibility. The witen would never have given its approval of such a choice. He was a foreigner and a bastard, either of which would have been sufficient to disqualify him as a candidate, much less the combination."

"Prior to King Edward's last illness, did you say anything, or take any action, to encourage King Edward to resolve the issue of his successor?"

"Yes, I did. I suggested that he try to find Edward the Exile, the last living person of the royal Saxon line."

"Did King Edward act on your suggestion?"

"Yes, he did. He sent Archbishop Ealdred to negotiate an entry to Hungary to seek out Edward the Exile. When those negotiations were eventually successful in 1057, I was ordered to escort Edward the Exile and his family back to England.

Edward the Exile was recognized by King Edward as an Aetheling, a throne-worthy person."

"Was Edward the Exile alive at the time of King Edward's death?"

"No, he was not. He had died within days of arriving in England."

"Upon Edward the Exile's death, did his son then become an Aetheling?"

"Technically, no, because his father had never been a king, but King Edward, essentially adopting Edgar, had him named an Aetheling. He was raised in the royal household as an Aetheling by Queen Edith."

At this point, Leofwine suggested to the Court that since he still had considerable inquiry of this witness, this might be a logical place to recess for the noon meal. Vos was in agreement with the suggestion and the noon recess was ordered, court to reconvene at two o'clock that afternoon.

Harold, with the afternoon testimony still to come, knew that food was not what he needed right now. What he needed was fresh air and a gallop to ease his tension and clear his mind. As soon as he arrived at his lodgings, he called for his groom to ready his horse. Mounting quickly, he set off at a gallop.

August 30th, 1066
Afternoon Session, Ghent, Flanders

Harold arrived at the court just as Leofwine was about to leave the courtroom so, unseen by Vos, he could pace outside. He was uncertain whether to be angry or worried at Harold's tardiness. Where was he? Would he return from wherever he was before the bailiff called the afternoon session to order? Had something happened to him?

When he finally arrived at the courthouse, much refreshed from his ride, and greeted his brother, Leofwine had a hard time deciding whether to punch him or hug him. He opted to hurry him into the courtroom, all the while asking where had he been, why was he so late.

Harold assured him he was fine. "I can cope with the afternoon's questions with equanimity and authority. I realize how difficult it is going to be to relive that afternoon in Bonneville-sur-Touques, but I also know it's critical the justices come to the same conclusion as did King Edward, Archbishop Ealdred and my confessor—that an oath not given freely and under duress, no matter on how many relics it was sworn, is of no effect and is non-binding!"

He and Leofwine had spent a great deal of time determining the presentation of the testimony of the actual oath-taking. There was a fine line between recognizing the sanctity of an oath to God, freely taken before his fellow man and an oath taken under real and present duress. The oath before God was the keystone of society. It should not, and could not, be taken lightly. These twelve justices must be persuaded Harold understood the gravity of such an oath, that falsely taken, his very soul was imperiled. But, he also had a duty to protect the lives of his men, his brother and nephew. William might call them 'guests' but in truth they were prisoners, fully under the control of and subject to the pleasure of William. And even though he and his men might go home, he had known that Wulfnoth would not. Harold also remembered the deadly fate of the former Count of Maine and his wife while they were 'guests' of Duke William.

Leofwine opened the afternoon session by asking King Harold to describe the circumstances just prior to the ceremony of knighting at Bonneville-sur-Tougues.

Harold responded that they had just returned from the successful campaign in Brittany and it was his understanding that Duke William was planning a feast in celebration and as a send-off to him and his men as they left for England on a boat that Duke William was finally providing. Duke William also gave him a suit of armor at that time and told him it was for saving the lives of his men and also so that he would be suitably attired when the duke knighted him.

"Had Duke William said anything about knighting you before he gave you the armor?" asked Leofwine.

"No, he had not."

"When did the duke first mention swearing an oath of fealty to him?"

"After the feasting, and after he had knighted me, an altar and casket were brought out and the duke said I was to swear an oath of fealty to him. I was surprised and a bit confused. I hesitated, not quite knowing what to do about it."

"Would you explain to the Court why you were hesitant and confused about taking an oath of fealty to William?"

"I was hesitant because I didn't see the point of an oath, or even the knighting, for that matter. I had already demonstrated that I was willing to help protect Duke William's interests in Normandy by joining him in the Brittany campaign. I had even saved the lives of two of his men at that time. And this was true even though my several requests for a boat to enable our return to England had fallen on deaf ears. My country and his duchy had long maintained ties of cooperation, so what purpose could my individual oath to William in Normandy serve?"

"You just mentioned that you also didn't see the point of the knighting. Why was that?" continued Leofwine.

"Well, first and foremost, I had no need or even any particular desire to become a knight of Normandy. At that time, in England, only King Edward was more powerful than I, and I actually had more personal wealth than King Edward. The lands I controlled in Wessex were three quarters the size of the duke's Normandy. If you considered my brothers holding as well, the Godwinesons controlled an area larger than Normandy. Knighting was a meaningless gesture to me, but if William wanted to do it, I would go along with it. If I was ever in Normandy again, it might be useful."

"What was the Duke's response to your hesitation?" queried Leofwine.

"He said it was a fitting conclusion to having knighted me and ordered me to swear an oath to be loyal to him."

"What was your reaction to that?" Leofwine guided the witness along a path of reasonable sounding reactions to an unexpected situation.

"It was his tone of voice when he said that I must swear the oath that made me realize William wasn't being just the genial host; he was very serious and insistent about my swearing an oath of fealty. It was at that point that I remembered Wulfnoth's warning to do whatever William wanted or he was a dead man. I remember looking at Harkon before I spoke. The look of fright on his face when it appeared I might not swear such an oath was a further reminder that we all were really William's prisoners —

"Objection, Your Honor, Vos nearly shouted, as he jumped to his feet. "There has been no foundation established to permit such a slanderous allegation into testimony. I move to strike the phrase 'William's prisoners' from the record." "Your Honor," Leofwine quickly countered, "the question asked for the witness's response to an order from the Plaintiff. It is relevant and admissible that he testifies as to his thoughts, emotions, and reactions which arose in response to that order." Chief Justice DiVinci took a quick poll of the other justices and announced, "objection overruled."

"What, if anything, did you do next?"

"Since our future was completely within Duke William's control, I said a silent prayer to God to forgive me if by taking this oath it was going to require me to do something at a later time that I could not in all conscience do. But I couldn't risk the lives of my men and my family by refusing."

"Sire, before you took the oath to be faithful to William's aims and purposes, did he indicate to you at any time that he intended to be King of England, or even that he thought he already was?" asked Leofwine in a very dogmatic voice.

Very distinctly and with authority, Harold answered with a resounding, "No, he did not."

"Duke William has alleged in this legal action that you are 'foresworn' of your oath to him and therefore unworthy to be King. Do you consider yourself foresworn?"

"No, I do not."

"Would you tell this Court why you do not believe that you are foresworn of your oath of fealty to Duke William?" asked Leofwine softly.

"First and foremost, because it was not freely given. I was forced to take the oath to insure the safety of Wulfnoth and my men. Secondly, although the words of the oath didn't say

225

it, it was understood that this oath was superseded by prior oaths of allegiance to our respective overlords, our kings. And finally, I didn't believe then, and I do not believe today, that loyalty or obligation to further Duke Williams pursuits extended beyond the boundaries of the lands over which he has a legal right to govern—namely Normandy."

Duke William, in his Complaint has alleged that you forced King Edward to name you as his successor. Did you ever in any way force King Edward to name you his successor?"

"Absolutely not. I had served Edward as my king faithfully until the night of his death. I continued to serve him after his death by carrying out his dying command, that I govern and protect England as her next king."

"Drawing your attention to the years after 1052, were you a close advisor to King Edward?"

"Yes, particularly after my father died in 1053, I was Edward's primary advisor and chief administrator."

"During those years, between 1052 and Christmastime 1065, did King Edward discuss with you the question of who would succeed him as King?"

"Yes, the subject came up numerous times during those years, but usually only in a very general way."

"What do you mean by 'in a general way'?"

"Well, for instance, if the Danes or other northern Scandinavian boats had made one of their periodic raids on our coast, Edward might mention if Harald Hardrada thought that he ought to be England's next king. He on occasion might make reference to Duke William, usually in the context of whether he was or was not providing shelter to his Viking relatives when they raided England's coastline. He might mutter a comment or so about the uproar when he had made a Norman, Robert of Jumières, Archbishop of Canterbury, but then go on to speak of something else. The most sustained conversations we had were when he decided to try to get Edward the Exile back to England from Hungary."

"Did King Edward during those years ever tell you that he had named William, Duke of Normandy as his heir?"

"No, he did not. I certainly would have questioned searching for Edward the Exile if he had ever told me he had done such a thing," answered Harold with certainty and vigor.

Pausing for a moment to give the justices a chance to fully absorb the impact of Harold's testimony, Leofwine then turned to the high bench, saying, I" have no further questions of this witness, Your Honors."

Chief Justice Di Vinci, glancing for a quick indication of approval from the other justices, announced that since it was late in the day, it seemed appropriate that Vicomte Vos start his cross-examination in the morning. Court was adjourned until nine o'clock the following morning. "The Witness is excused until that time."

The bailiff called for all to rise as the justices filed out. Harold and Leofwine carefully avoided each other's glances for fear they might be seen to be as jubilant as they were that their timetable had worked out. The justices would have the evening to mull over Harold's testimony without any adverse input from William's counsel. Granted, it gave Vos more time to prepare his cross-examination, but the brothers had determined in their strategy sessions that that was preferable to having a challenging cross-examination start right on the heels of Harold's direct testimony.

Vicomte Vos was not unhappy with the Court's decision to leave cross-examination for the following day. Despite the impact of leaving direct testimony unchallenged, he welcomed the extra time the overnight hours gave him to create the most effective cross-examination he was able to devise. While he and William enjoyed the ride to Count Baldwin's castle after the long day in court, he told William, "You will need to spend some time with me this evening going over Harold's testimony. Two recollections of the testimony should ensure that my cross-examination covers all the important points of his testimony."

August 31st, 1066
Day 10 of Trial, Ghent, Flanders

Starting what would hopefully be the last day of testimony, Harold Godwineson once again settled himself in the witness stand. He was confident that he would withstand successfully any cross-examination that Richard Vos could put to him.

Vos also was confident that he could seriously challenge the defendant's direct testimony. He had reviewed his notes of Harold's examination at length during the previous evening, and had a clear picture in his mind of what he needed to do today. He started to approach the witness and suddenly hesitated. He had just had a horrible thought. How was he to address the witness? Pretending he had forgotten something at counsel table, he slowly retraced his steps. His mind raced among options. William would have his head if he addressed the witness as Sire or Your Majesty. Since he had been consecrated and crowned King, he was no longer the Earl of Wessex, so the title of earl was no longer appropriate. Realizing he could stall no longer, he picked up some random papers from the table and re-approached the witness.

Hoping that it would not raise an objection from Leofwine, he asked, "My Lord, yesterday you testified that you had faithfully served your king, King Edward, did you not?"

"I did."

"Yet in 1051, you joined your father in rebellion against your king's orders, breaking your oath of allegiance to King Edward didn't you?"

"I did join my father in leaving England, but it was not a rebellion against King Edward. If anyone failed to honor an oath, King Edward did by failing to obey the laws and rule justly and in accordance with law."

Vos, with a look of surprise and incredulous tone of voice, asked, "Are you telling this Honorable Court that joining someone who has refused to carry out a king's order and had fled to avoid arrest is not an act of rebellion—is that your testimony?"

"It is not an act of rebellion to refuse to obey an illegal order. It is not a rebellion to avoid taking up arms against your sovereign by leaving the country," answered Harold quietly.

"Yet when you returned to England the following year, it was at the head of armed men, on a march to London to confront the king, isn't that true?" barked Vos.

"No, it is not. My brother and I returned from Ireland, and the people of Wessex voluntarily joined us to show their support. They were not armed men, nor did we 'march' to London. Any confrontation with King Edward, if any, was solely between my father and King Edward."

"Would you have this court believe that this mass exodus from England of the Godwine family in 1051 had nothing to do with you, or your loyalty to your king? Is that your testimony?" asked Vos, the disbelief evident on his face.

"Naturally, I supported my father but not by taking up arms against my king. I left England with my brother so the King could not use me against my father."

Having gained all he could from this line of questioning, Vicomte Vos changed the subject. "Is it your testimony that in exchange for the oath of fealty you swore to Duke William, you gained no benefice?"

"Yes," answered Harold, shortly, adding nothing more."

"You were provided a boat to return to England, weren't you?"

"At best, most of us were provided transportation, not a boat," said Harold, emphasizing the word. "We were ferried by a Norman boat with a Norman crew to England. The boat and crew then returned to Normandy. It cost Duke William nothing but a few days of his sailor's time and was an isolated event. Certainly nothing anyone would call a long term benefice."

"Well, certainly rescue from Count Guy's imprisonment, was a benefice received, wasn't it?"

Harold straightened in the witness box and looking directly at his examiner answered, "No."

"You were delivered from the prison of a man who would demand payment for your release, treated as a guest by Duke William, and yet you do not consider it a benefice—is that your testimony?"

"Yes. If Count Guy—"

Vos interrupted, "You have answered the question, there is no question before you."

Loefwine rose addressing the Court. "Your Honor, the witness was attempting to explain his testimony as requested by counsel. He should be permitted to fully answer as to what his testimony was, and meant."

A quick survey of the justices and Chief Justice Di Vinci ruled that the witness could answer but to keep it relevant.

Harold continued, "If Count Guy had continued to hold me, a ransom demand would have been made and paid. I would likely have been back in England within a month or so, not the almost six months I was detained in Normandy. I never asked Duke William to 'rescue' me, but if a debt was owed for doing so, it was paid by my aid and that of my men in relieving the siege at Dol. Several of my men were injured in that action which befitted only Duke William. And I saved the lives of two of his men from drowning in quicksand on the way back to Normandy."

"I suppose it would be fair to say that you don't consider having been knighted by Duke William a benefice either, wouldn't it?" asked Vos, sarcastically.

"I don't consider it to be of any benefit to me. I didn't ask for it and had no need of it then or now. At that time, I was the most powerful earl in England. Of what value is a Norman knighthood compared to that?" Harold ignored Vos' sarcasm and essentially asked the justices his question.

Vos, in a different tone of voice as he attempted to regain control of the questioning, focused on Harold's admission of power within England, asked, "It would be fair to say, wouldn't it, that as the most powerful earl in England, you had a great deal of influence with King Edward?"

"Yes."

"And he took your advice on many matters, didn't he?"

"Yes."

"It would be fair to say that during the last few years of his reign, he gave you free rein to decide many state matters, without his direct input, wouldn't it?"

"Yes."

"And when he fell ill, with his trust in you and knowing you could take the throne by force, if needed, you were able to convince him that England would suffer if he didn't designate you as his heir, weren't you?"

"No, I did no such thing," answered Harold staring straight at Vos..

Vos went on, accusing Harold, "And as soon as he died, before anyone had a chance to dispute your actions, you and your brothers saw to it that the Witenagemot met and approved you as the successor to King Edward, didn't you?"

"No, the Witen met because everyone was already in London for the Christmas festivities and the consecration of Edward's new Westminster Abbey. There also were enough earls and prelates and thegns gathered that even combined, the Godwines didn't have a controlling vote, even if they had tried, which they didn't."

Chief Justice Di Vinci intervened at this point to say that since it was apparent that the Vicomte's examination would not be completed for a while, this would be a reasonable place to take the noon recess. Court would reconvene at two o'clock that afternoon.

The noon meal was a quiet one for all the parties. William was occupied with calculating schedules for his men and ships in the event of a contrary decision.

Vos still had to try to crack King Harold's confident demeanor and show him for the usurper he was. But he was not all that confident he would be any more successful in the afternoon than he had been this morning.

Leofwine, Harkon and Harold were quietly optimistic Harold would continue to thwart Vos during the afternoon's examination, as he had during the morning. Leofwine thought the afternoon session might be fairly short if Harold could maintain his position of calm and authoritative answers. Based on Harold's testimony so far, Leofwine doubted that he would have much, if any, re-direct examination.

As expected, Richard Vos spent the better part of the afternoon trying to shake King Harold's testimony. trying to trap the witness into testimony of misdoings: of lying, of undue influence, of false swearing, of callous ingratitude and abuse of his power to have himself crowned as king. None of his ploys were successful. Harold maintained his calm demeanor. Gone were the days of doubts and turmoil over his oath of fealty. He had resolved those issues and was firm in the rightness of his actions, in his duty to protect England and belief that William was a very real and present danger to England's welfare.

There were perhaps several minor points Leofwine could have cleared up with re-direct but on balance, he decided that the regal demeanor with which Harold had cloaked himself all day, was best left undisturbed in the justices' minds. When Vos announced he had no further questions, Leofwine also said he had no re-direct, and the Defendant rested.

There being no further witnesses, the Court set ten o'clock Monday morning for closing arguments to be heard. Court was adjourned until that time.

The parties left the courtroom, each immersed in his own thoughts now that the testimonial part of the trial had ended. Harold, striding freely and surely to their lodgings, was relieved that his testimony was over and satisfied he had done all that he could do to honor King Edward's charge to keep England safe and secure. Although still anxious about the eventual decision the justices would reach, his part was over. He could only help Leofwine fine-tune his closing argument. The final act of the trial was up to Leofwine. He fervently said a prayer that it would not also be the final act of his kingship.

Harkon, with the optimism of youth, chatted nonstop as they walked from the courthouse. Recalling the highlights of Harold's testimony, he was convinced the justices could come to only one decision, that Harold was innocent of any wrongdoing and William was a liar. Harold was clearly relieved that the testimony was over with, but still concerned about the final outcome. *But, how could he not be? His whole future, and most likely that of England, was at stake.*

Leofwine, was walking along, silently, letting Harkon's chatter just flow over him. He was already listing in his mind the arguments he needed to include in his closing statement. It would be his final chance to steer the justices firmly in the direction of a judgment in favor of Harold, and he needed to be sure he used his ammunition wisely.

As William and Richard Vos rode to Count Baldwin's castle, William's thoughts spun in his mind of how, if at all, could he reach the justices to ensure a decision in his favor. He did not personally know any of the justices so a casual meeting of friends, even if it were possible, was out of the question. He was having no success coming up with a way to help insure a judgment favorable to him. However, the thought of his men and ships awaiting only his order (and favorable winds) buoyed his thoughts considerably. Whatever outcome the justices decided upon, he still had his Plan B. As the successful soldier he was, he had the utmost confidence in a favorable outcome to his Plan B!

Richard Vos, Vicomte de Counches en Ouche, was just as glad that William seemed occupied with his own thoughts and not inclined to conversation on the ride to Count Baldwin's. He knew what a formidable task he had ahead of him to present a convincing closing argument to the Court. *If only Archbishop Robert were still alive. His testimony could have made all the difference. Even if the English Earls had been alive. Granted, they would be hostile witnesses, but not that fond of the Godwine family. And under oath, they would likely have told the truth of Edward's selection of Duke William. Of course, to be honest, there would have been the risk that they might have also added testimony that he didn't want, but it would have been a risk worth taking, had it only been available. Well, at least, there are two days to put a closing together.*

September 3d, 1066
Day 11 of Trial, Ghent, Flanders

Harkon took his usual seat at the rear of the courtroom. *We'll be here only one more time. And that will be the real day of reckoning, when we hear the Justice's decision. Have they already made up their minds or will today's closing arguments actually make a difference? How long will it take them to decide? The longer the better for Harold. The closer it gets to winter, the less likely William could wage any military action against England.*

Harkon suddenly straightened. *But if William loses, what will happen to Wulfnoth? What if William takes out his anger at losing on him? Will I ever see him again?* His thoughts were interrupted by the bailiff calling the Court to order and the entry of the justices to the high bench.

Chief Justice Di Vinci addressed the parties. "Is counsel ready to begin their closing arguments to the Court?"

Both Vos and Leofwine stood and answered that they were ready.

Turning to plaintiff's table, Justice Di Vinci said, "You may proceed Vicomte Vos."

"Your Honors, you have heard the Plaintiff's testimony of how at a young age, Edward of England's trauma of exile was assuaged by a warm welcome into the family of his Norman relatives. For approximately twenty-four years, during most of the formative years of his life, King Edward was fed, sheltered and raised as a son by the Dukes of Normandy. In his later years, when it became obvious that he and his Queen would not be blessed with children, naturally he would turn to his other family, his Noman one, as his probable heir. And this is precisely what he did. As Archbishop Robert of Jumières reported to Duke William, King Edward named William his heir, to be the next king of England. In accordance with English law, he obtained the approval of his counselors of the witen, that they would support his choice when the time came to do so. King Edward even took the son and nephew of Earl Godwine as hostages to ensure that the most powerful Earl in England stayed true to his word to be loyal to, and support, his king. King Edward sent his friend and advisor Bishop Robert of Jumières to inform Duke William of his decision, confirming their earlier discussions. It is important to note that the Defendant, in his testimony, has not denied the testimony of Archbishop Robert's report to Duke William regarding King Edward's designation of Duke William as his heir.

"As the testimony has shown, King Edward was well aware of the custom of investing one's heir with the title which was to be his, while the titleholder continued to live. He had still been in exile in Normandy when his cousin Duke Robert I had his son William, the Plaintiff herein, named and invested as Duke of Normandy while Duke Robert was still alive. He fully understood the gravity of such a *post obitum* gift and its irrevocability. Upon the death of Duke Robert, young as he was, William was acknowledged as the successor to his father. His Norman vicomtes, comtes and prelates kept their word to Duke Robert to support his choice of his heir and acknowledged William as the next duke. As Duke William told you, King Edward sent his close friend and advisor, the Archbishop of Canterbury, Robert of Jumiéres, to personally convey his decision to have Duke William as his heir.

"Some years later, when the Defendant's voyage across the Channel ended so disastrously upon the shores of Count Guy's lands, Duke William went to the aid of the Defendant, then Earl of Wessex, and rescued him from the prison of Count Guy. He brought Earl Harold and his men to Normandy as his guests. Not to demand ransom, not to keep him as a prisoner. No, he and his men were treated as the honored guests they were. Subsequently, in friendship and brotherhood, Earl Harold even joined in a campaign to rescue one of Duke William's vassals from a siege.

"In celebration of this successful campaign, and the help given in friendship, Duke William honored Earl Harold by knighting him, even giving him a handsome suit of armor for the occasion. And aware of the honor awarded him, the Defendant, in the presence of his men and those of Duke William, freely and in full faith, his hands on a bible and holy relics, pledged his support and allegiance to Duke William and his causes. There is no doubt that the Defendant swore such an oath. You heard the testimony of Comte Robert, who personally witnessed the event. Nor has the Defendant denied taking such an oath. But two years later, when the time came to honor that solemn pledge before man and God, did the Defendant keep faith with Duke William and support him in his rightful claim as heir to King Edward? No, Your Honors, he did not! Despite his solemn pledge, the Earl of Wessex, willfully exercising all of his awesome power, second only to that of the dying King, manipulated the men of England to his own benefit to become the next King of England! In blatant disregard of his prior oath of fealty to Duke William, he not only failed to support the legitimate claim of Duke William, but he usurped the throne for himself.

"A man foresworn of such a solemn oath before God cannot be trusted to be the leader of a country. His word, his bond, his very integrity is worthless in the face of his breach of his oath. Who could trust him to rule with justice and according to law when he wouldn't keep his word to God?

"With it clear that the Defendant had not observed his oath to Duke William and God, it was only natural and fitting that the duke would seek the advice and support of the Church in this matter. This was an oath sworn before God, on holy relics; something that would clearly be within the purview of the Church. If, after hearing from the duke's delegation, his Holiness could not see his way to openly support one of his children over another, neither did he condemn any efforts that Duke William might make to rectify the wrong done to him. In fact, as Archdeacon Gilbert testified, His Holiness sent a ring containing a saint's hair to show his understanding of and sympathy for the Duke's position. There has been no showing by the Defendant that His Holiness has shown such public or private support for the Defendant.

"But I ask you, Your Honors, even if you accept that King Edward made a dying declaration appointing the Defendant as his successor, even if that really happened, how could the Defendant in all honesty and good faith accept it? He had taken an oath before God. He had already committed himself to support Duke William's causes. He was not eligible to claim the throne in contravention of that sworn oath of support and loyalty. And if he is not eligible, then King Edward's *post obitum* gift is still in effect. William Duke of Normandy is the rightful heir of King Edward and England's lawful king."

Thanking the Justices for their attention, Vos returned to counsel table and the Court gave permission for Earl Godwinson to proceed on behalf of the Defendant.

"Your Honors, you have heard the Vicomte of Onches' eloquent summary of the heinous and wrongful actions supposedly engaged in by the Defendant and how those actions have deprived the Duke of Normandy of that which is rightfully his, namely, the throne of England. And an eloquent story it was. However, that is all it is—a story. It is made up of supposition, innuendo and wishful thinking, with little or no basis in fact. And what facts were presented to you, are irrelevant to the duke's alleged right to be King of England. Let me review the facts or rather the lack thereof, as the Plaintiff would have you believe them.

"The plaintiff claims that the late King Edward made an irrevocable *post obitum* gift of the crown of England to him. By the testimony of the Plaintiff's own Norman prelate, Father Lanfranc, first and foremost for such a gift to be irrevocable, the gift must be perfected. Nowhere in any testimony, either as presented by the Plaintiff or by the duke's own secretary, was there any evidence presented that the alleged *post* obitum gift was ever perfected. No testimony was presented that any tangible evidence of the alleged gift was ever offered or delivered to the Plaintiff. He received an oral message from Archbishop Robert that such a gift was made. That was it! Nothing was given him, even symbolically, to represent such a gift. He was merely told that King Edward has said he was his heir. By Father Lanfranc's own definition, the elements required to perfect an irrevocable gift and make it binding under law were conspicuous by their absence. While the donee need not be present to receive and accept the gift, if there was a surrogate—as was Archbishop Robert in this case— then the surrogate must perform all of the necessary actions required for perfection. Archbishop Robert did not perform any actions, symbolic or otherwise. He merely told the duke of King Edward's words. The Plaintiff's own secretary was present when Duke William was told of King Edward's alleged words. His testimony was that nothing was exchanged nor presented to the Plaintiff except words—mere words. Even assuming that the 'words' had, in fact, been said, without perfection of the gift, those 'words' were no more than a pious wish, unenforceable in law.

"As important as the perfection of a gift may be, there is an even more stringent requirement for the giving of a gift. The donor must have title to and/or be in rightful possession of the *res,* the thing of the gift. This aspect of a gift is so basic a fundamental that it scarcely needed Father Lanfranc's scholarly testimony to bring it to the Court's attention. Given that all the lands of Normandy were given to the Plaintiff's forebears by the King of France, as a Norman, the Plaintiff can perhaps be forgiven for assuming such was also the case in England. However, as you heard by the testimony of Archbishop Ealdred and Earl Morcar, such is not the case in England. The king does not own all the lands of England, nor does he have the right or authority to dispose of the kingdom as if it were his personal chattel. Much of the lands of northern England, those of the so-called Danelaw are titled to the owners as a result of invasion, conquest and settlement by Danish Vikings. Upon taking the throne, King Edward, like the English kings before him, took an oath to rule justly and in accordance with law and custom, to respect the traditional rights and holdings of his people. He took an oath to be a just and legal leader of the English.

"His earls and prelate and thegns also agreed to be loyal and law-abiding subjects to their lord. King Edward could and did express by his dying declaration, the person he chose to be his successor, but that alone did not make that designated person the king. Until and unless the earls, prelate and thegns of the witenagemot agreed to accept such a person as their king and pledged their allegiance to him, there would be no consecration of that person as king. These are the facts of English law, testified to by Archbishop Ealdred, and Earl Morcar.

"Although raised in Normandy, King Edward was English. He reigned for nearly twenty-five years. To suggest he knowingly made an illegal *post* obitum gift, some fifteen years before his death, while he was still hale and hearty and capable of fathering a son, stretches the truth beyond belief.

"The other main support upon which the Plaintiff built his case, is that King Harold was ineligible to become the king because he was foresworn of his oath of fealty to Duke William. But what did that oath really mean? The Defendant does not deny that he took an oath of fealty to Duke William. Even if it had been freely given, which as you heard the testimony it was not, and even if there had been any reciprocity of obligations, which there was not, exactly what was the Defendant obligated to do by his oath? According to Bishop Fulbert's exposition of the duties and obligations involved, as set forth in his letter entered into evidence, the Defendant was to be loyal to the duke, to help further his legal aims and endeavors and to give him sound advice regarding matters within the legitimate purview of the duke. In other words, Norman matters, not English. Nor was he obligated to prefer Duke William as lord over his prior-acknowledged liege lord, King Edward. His first duty was to follow his King's instructions and wishes. First he was to care for and protect England.

"The second important aspect of the issue of whether King Harold is foresworn of his oath of fealty is that any such oath must be given by the oath-taker of his own free will and without duress of any kind. Is it believable that as the most powerful Earl in England, second in power only to the king and acknowledged by his peers as *subregulus*, the Defendant would choose to spend almost six months as the 'guest' of Duke William? That he would tarry thus, away from his duties as earl and the king's chief advisor? I respectfully suggest to Your Honors that it is not. As King Harold testified, he had on many occasions requested to be allowed to return to England but had been refused. Not until Duke William chose to allow it was such return permitted. And even then, the return was allowed only under conditions established by the Plaintiff.

"Those conditions were that he take an oath of fealty to the Plaintiff and that the defendant's youngest brother remain a captive of the Duke. Wulfnoth was a captive, not a hostage! The man for whose conduct he was surety was long since dead. This Court heard the Defendant's testimony: he sought Wulfnoth's release, not to place him in further captivity. As King Harold told you, he and King Edward were well aware of the sudden and unexplained deaths of King Edward's nephew, the Count of Maine, and his wife while in the 'custody' of Duke William. King Harold, responsible for the lives of his men and his brother remaining under Duke William's control, knew he had no choice but to do the duke's bidding and swear an oath to him. Was there duress? Of course there was. Was such an oath sworn to as King Harold's free act and deed? Of course not.

"This Honorable Court heard the testimony of Father Gilbert that His Holiness 'couldn't prefer one of his children over another' as the reason why the Pope could only privately support the Defendant's claims. On the surface, this seems as if it might be a reasonable explanation. But is it? Isn't it far more likely that the Pope could not openly ignore cannons promulgated by legally empowered legates and adopted by the secular powers of the land as law? Could the Church just ignore its own ban forbidding inheritances by bastards?

"This court has heard the testimony regarding the procedures for empowering a successor king under English law. Would, or even could, the Church say to a country's leader—accepted by its people as chosen in accordance with law and subsequently anointed by God's representative on earth, an

Archbishop of the Church—'sorry, I as Pope have decided that you are no longer sanctified as King of the English. I've chosen someone else. No, of course not. Even such a thought is ludicrous! The Pope knows, as does everyone here in this august hall, once there has been a consecration of the physical being as king, he is the King! Even in exile, he is still a king. Only death removes that consecrated mantle. Yet, that is just what Duke William asked the Pope to do. When His Holiness rightfully declined to take any such action, the Plaintiff turned to this Court. He is asking this Honorable Court to depose a Church anointed King, chosen by the dying declaration of an anointed king and unanimously accepted by the English people, from his throne. All on the basis of the unsupported testimony of the man who would be the new king. Duke William's ambition and wishful thinking does not change the facts. There was no perfected *post obitum* gift. There was no freely given oath of loyalty by the defendant with reciprocal obligations by each party. There was no 'usurpation' of England's throne; the Defendant was chosen in accordance with English tradition and legal procedures. With the exchange of oaths between the agreed upon successor and his subjects, Harold of Wessex became King of England. Consecration by a Prince of the Church confirmed Harold as God's irrevocable, anointed ruler and caretaker of the English people."

Thanking the Court for their attention, Leofwine concluded his argument and returned to counsel table.

Chief Justice Di Vinci announced that the Court would take the matter under advisement. When a decision was reached, counsel would be notified of the time and date when court would reconvene to hear the Court's decision.

September 17th, 1066
Ghent, Flanders

The tension in the stately courtroom was palpable. Harkon could barely control himself enough to take his seat, when he all he really wanted to do was pace the floor while awaiting the Justices. The parties appeared less affected by the significance of their presence today in this impressive chamber, but mainly because they were older and had had time to develop a leader's aura of detachment and calm control, not matter what was at stake.

The 'stakes' in this matter were certainly high!

Whump! Whump! Whump! The contact resonated within the stately chambers as the court bailiff struck the floor with his staff, after the final blow crying the traditional invocation, "Oyez, Oyez, Oyez. All persons having business before the Honorable, the Justices of the Court of Justice of the Association of International Communities are admonished to draw near and give their attention, for the Court is now sitting. God save the Association of International Communities and this Honorable Court."

The twelve judges, habited in their black robes and white lace jabots, created an aura of stateliness and morality as they solemnly filed into the cathedral-like courtroom and took their places at the long, high bench, crowned by the stained glass windows.

The parties and the International communities would now learn the legal consequences, if any, of the Earl of Wessex's oath of fealty; and the validity of Duke William's claims; whether King Harold II would remain King of England.

The Chief Justice opened the session. "this Honorable Court, after solemn deliberation of the evidence and testimony presented by the parties, giving due respect to all applicable laws this matter, has reached a decision in this matter.

"The Court has accepted as fact the allegation King Edward nominated the plaintiff Duke William of Normandy, to be his heir in 1051. The defendant King Harold II of England presented no evidence or testimony which would refute this claim by the Plaintiff. The Court finds however, that the relevant fact concerning this nomination is not that it was made, but whether it was made as a *post obitum* gift. The testimony of Plaintiff's witness Abbot Lanfranc established that there are criteria which must be fulfilled to make a valid *post obitum* gift. Three criteria in particular are necessary-right of ownership of the *res* of the gift, perfection of delivery of it and its revocability. The Plaintiff has failed to produce any evidence that King Edward had the requisite right, title or interest in and to all the lands of England or the sole right to control the succession to the throne of England. The Defendant has established by credible testimony that King Edward did not have such sole rights. Regarding the remaining criteria, revocability was established by the Defendant's testimony if King Edward had a son and several of Plaintiff's witnesses testified ass to the role of the Witenagemot in the legitimacy of a new king. Therefore, this Court holds that the alleged promise by King Edward to William of Normandy that the said William would be his heir, while it likely was made, is not a *post obitum* gift and is not irrevocable. The Court further holds that the procedures which the leading earls, prelate and thegns of England followed in acclaiming the Defendant as its King were in accordance with English laws and custom.

Plaintiff has also alleged that as a result of Defendant's oath of fealty to the plaintiff, the defendant is foresworn and ineligible to assume the mantle of kingship. Both parties provided this Court with evidence and testimony of the meaning of such an oath and its obligations. Our society is replete with such oaths, many of which are overlapping and conflicting in their obligations. However, there are common denominators of all. The obligations are linear, reciprocal and within national borders. In this instance the plaintiff has attempted to stretch the boundaries of an oath to include a binding promise of action by the defendant in another nation while omitting any reciprocity of obligations by the plaintiff in his territory. Further, it nearly goes without saying that any sacred oath, whether on holy relics of not, must be freely given. This Court holds that such freely given consent to an oath of fealty was not given by King Harold. The retention of Defendant's youngest brother by Plaintiff even to this day is ample evidence of the coercion by the Defendant.

The final issue considered by the Court, although not strictly necessary in view of the above holdings, is that of the jurisdiction and/or moral right of this Court to dethrone a consecrated, anointed king. The testimony clearly established that only the defendant challenged the succession to the throne of England of Harold of Wessex. The leaders of England acknowledged the legitimacy of the process and pledged their loyalty the new King. This Court holds that it has no jurisdiction to overturn such a legal process. Further, once that legal process is finalized and sanctified by the servant of God on earth, once the King is acclaimed, it is beyond the power of this or any other court to undo.

WHEREFORE, this Court gives judgment for the Defendant, King Harold II of England.

This decision is the unanimous decision of the Court.

###

Connect with Me Online

My Blog: http:// www.susansmaire.com

www.ingramcontent.com/pod-product-compliance
Lightning Source LLC
Chambersburg PA
CBHW022004170626

46808CB00001B/282